WHEN GOD LAUGHS

Prometheus's Literary Classics Series

JACK LONDON

WHEN GOD LAUGHS

■

LITERARY CLASSICS

 **Prometheus Books**

59 John Glenn Drive
Amherst, New York 14228-2197

Published 2005 by Prometheus Books

Inquiries should be addressed to
Prometheus Books
59 John Glenn Drive
Amherst, New York 14228–2197

VOICE: 716–691–0133, EXT. 207; FAX: 716–564–2711.
WWW.PROMETHEUSBOOKS.COM

09 08 07 06 05   5 4 3 2 1

Library of Congress Cataloging-in-Publication Data

London, Jack, 1876–1916.
    When God laughs : and other stories / Jack London.
        p. cm. — (Literary classics)
    Originally published: London : Macmillan, 1911.
    ISBN 1–59102–244–4 (pbk. : alk. paper)
    I. Title. II. Literary classics (Amherst, N.Y.)

PS353.O46 W+
813'.52—dc22

                                        2004020383

Printed in the United States of America on acid-free paper.

Born as John Griffith Chaney in San Francisco on January 12, 1876, JACK LONDON grew up in a world witnessing the settlement of the last frontier. He was raised by his mother and his stepfather, whose surname, London, he took. Many of the details of London's early life remain speculative, but as an adolescent he adopted the nickname Jack, and at the age of fourteen he quit school to seek adventure.

During his travels, London witnessed depression-era conditions across the country and was jailed in Niagara Falls, New York, for vagrancy. By many accounts, this thirty-day imprisonment served as a turning point in his life. He decided to educate himself and pursue a career in writing. However, searching for adventure was to remain a theme throughout the course of London's life and his work. He worked as a seaman, a prospector in the first Klondike gold rush, a newspaper correspondent during the Russo-Japanese War, and a war correspondent in Mexico in 1914.

London's stories, romantic adventures with realistic settings and characters, based on his firsthand experiences as a high adventurer, began to appear first in the *Overland Monthly*. However, he is best known for his Klondike tales, which are captivating, exciting, and often brutal. *The Call of the Wild* (1903), about a tame dog who eventually leads a pack of wolves, is one of the best animal stories ever written. Among his other works are *The Sea-Wolf* (1904), *White Fang* (1905), *The Iron Heel* (1907), *When God Laughs* (1911), and *Smoke Bellew* (1912).

As one of the highest paid and most publicized figures of his day, London used his fame to speak up for the underdog against justice and oppression, including the savagery and torture of prison life. He lectured on and endorsed socialism, women's suffrage, and eventually, prohibition.

The last decade of London's life was marked by physical ailments, including a kidney disease of unknown origin. He died at the age of forty of gastrointestinal uremic poisoning, which caused kidney failure on November 22, 1916. Nevertheless, during his short career, he had published more than fifty books, including novels, nonfiction works, and volumes of short stories, as well as hundreds of articles, essays, and reviews.

CONTENTS

WHEN GOD LAUGHS

WHEN GOD LAUGHS

(WITH COMPLIMENTS
TO HARRY COWELL)

"The gods, the gods are stronger; time
Falls down before them, all men's knees
Bow, all men's prayers and sorrows climb
Like incense toward them; yea, for these
Are gods, Felise."

Carquinez had relaxed finally. He stole a glance at the rattling windows, looked upward at the beamed roof, and listened for a moment to the savage roar of the southeaster as it caught the bungalow in its bellowing jaws. Then he held his glass between him and the fire and laughed for joy through the golden wine.

"It is beautiful," he said. "It is sweetly sweet. It is a woman's wine, and it was made for gray-robed saints to drink."

"We grow it on our own warm hills," I said, with

pardonable California pride. "You rode up yesterday through the vines from which it was made."

It was worth while to get Carquinez to loosen up. Nor was he ever really himself until he felt the mellow warmth of the wine singing in his blood. He was an artist, it is true, always an artist; but somehow, sober, the high pitch and lilt went out of his thought-processes and he was prone to be as deadly dull as a British Sunday—not dull as other men are dull, but dull when measured by the sprightly wight that Monte Carquinez was when he was really himself.

From all this it must not be inferred that Carquinez, who is my dear friend and dearer comrade, was a sot. Far from it. He rarely erred. As I have said, he was an artist. He knew when he had enough, and enough, with him, was equilibrium—the equilibrium that is yours and mine when we are sober.

His was a wise and instinctive temperateness that savored of the Greek. Yet he was far from Greek. "I am Aztec, I am Inca, I am Spaniard," I have heard him say. And in truth he looked it, a compound of strange and ancient races, what of his swarthy skin and the asymmetry and primitiveness of his features. His eyes, under massively arched brows, were wide apart and black with the blackness that is barbaric, while before them was perpetually falling down a great black mop of hair through which he gazed like a roguish satyr from a thicket. He invariably wore a soft flannel shirt under his velvet-corduroy jacket, and his necktie was red. This latter stood for the red flag (he had once lived with the socialists of Paris), and it symbolized the blood and brotherhood of man. Also, he had never been known to wear anything on his head save a leather-banded sombrero. It was even rumored that he had been born with this particular piece of headgear. And in my experience it was provocative of nothing short of sheer delight to see that Mexican sombrero hailing a cab in Piccadilly or storm-tossed in the crush for the New York Elevated.

As I have said, Carquinez was made quick by wine—"as the clay was made quick when God breathed the breath of life into it," was his way of saying it. I confess that he was blasphemously intimate with God; and I must add that there was no blasphemy in him. He was at all times honest, and, because he was compounded of paradoxes, greatly misunderstood by those who did not know him. He could be as elementally raw at times as a screaming savage; and at other times as delicate as a maid, as subtle as a Spaniard. And—well, was he not Aztec? Inca? Spaniard?

And now I must ask pardon for the space I have given him. (He is my friend, and I love him.) The house was shaking to the storm, as he drew closer to the fire and laughed at it through his wine. He looked at me, and by the added lustre of his eye, and by the alertness of it, I knew that at last he was pitched in his proper key.

"And so you think you've won out against the gods?" he demanded.

"Why the gods?"

"Whose will but theirs has put satiety upon man?" he cried.

"And whence the will in me to escape satiety?" I asked triumphantly.

"Again the gods," he laughed. "It is their game we play. They deal and shuffle all the cards...and take the stakes. Think not that you have escaped by fleeing from the mad cities. You with your vine-clad hills, your sunsets and your sunrises, your homely fare and simple round of living!

"I've watched you ever since I came. You have not won. You have surrendered. You have made terms with the enemy. You have made confession that you are tired. You have flown the white flag of fatigue. You have nailed up a notice to the effect that life is ebbing down in you. You have run away from life. You have played a trick, shabby trick. You have balked at the game. You refuse to play. You have thrown your cards under the table and run away to hide, here amongst your hills."

He tossed his straight hair back from his flashing eyes, and scarcely interrupted to roll a long, brown, Mexican cigarette.

"But the gods know. It is an old trick. All the generations of man have tried it...and lost. The gods know how to deal with such as you. To pursue is to possess, and to possess is to be sated. And so you, in your wisdom, have refused any longer to pursue. You have elected surcease. Very well. You will become sated with surcease. You say you have escaped satiety! You have merely bartered it for senility. And senility is another name for satiety. It is satiety's masquerade. Bah!"

"But look at me!" I cried.

Carquinez was ever a demon for haling one's soul out and making rags and tatters of it.

He looked me witheringly up and down.

"You see no signs" I challenged.

"Decay is insidious," he retorted. "You are rotten ripe."

I laughed and forgave him for his very deviltry. But he refused to be forgiven.

"Do I not know?" he asked. "The gods always win. I have watched men play for years what seemed a winning game. In the end they lost."

"Don't you ever make mistakes?" I asked.

He blew many meditative rings of smoke before replying.

"Yes, I was nearly fooled, once. Let me tell you. There was Marvin Fiske. You remember him? And his Dantesque face and poet's soul, singing his chant of the flesh, the very priest of Love? And there was Ethel Baird, whom also you must remember."

"A warm saint," I said.

"That is she! Holy as Love, and sweeter! Just a woman, made for love; and yet—how shall I say?—drenched through with holiness as your own air here is with the perfume of flowers. Well, they married. They played a hand with the gods—"

"And they won, they gloriously won!" I broke in.

Carquinez looked at me pityingly, and his voice was like a funeral bell.

"They lost. They supremely, colossally lost."

"But the world believes otherwise," I ventured coldly.

"The world conjectures. The world sees only the face of things. But I know. Has it ever entered your mind to wonder why she took the veil, buried herself in that dolorous convent of the living dead?"

"Because she loved him so, and when he died ..."

Speech was frozen on my lips by Carquinez's sneer.

"A pat answer," he said, "machine-made like a piece of cotton-drill. The world's judgment! And much the world knows about it. Like you, she fled from life. She was beaten. She flung out the white flag of fatigue. And no beleaguered city ever flew that flag in such bitterness and tears.

"Now I shall tell you the whole tale, and you must believe me, for I know. They had pondered the problem of satiety. They loved Love. They knew to the uttermost farthing the value of Love. They loved him so well that they were fain to keep him always, warm and athrill in their hearts. They welcomed his coming; they feared to have him depart.

"Love was desire, they held, a delicious pain. He was ever seeking easement, and when he found that for which he sought, he died. Love denied was Love alive; Love granted was Love deceased. Do you follow me? They saw it was not the way of life to be hungry for what it has. To eat and still be hungry—man has never accomplished that feat. The problem of satiety. That is it. To have and to keep the sharp famine-edge of appetite at the groaning board. This was their problem, for they loved Love. Often did they discuss it, with all Love's sweet ardors brimming in their eyes; his ruddy blood spraying their cheeks; his voice playing in and out with their voices, now hiding as a tremolo in their throats, and again shading a tone with that ineffable tenderness which he alone can utter.

"How do I know all this? I saw—much. More I learned from her diary. This I found in it, from Fiona Macleod: 'For, truly, that wandering voice, that twilight-whisper, that breath so dewy-sweet, that flame-winged lute-player whom none sees but for a moment, in a rainbow-shimmer of joy, or a sudden lightning-flare of passion, this exquisite mystery we call Amor, comes, to some rapt visionaries at least, not with a song upon the lips that all may hear, or with blithe viol of public music, but as one wrought by ecstasy, dumbly eloquent with desire.'

"How to keep the flame-winged lute-player with his dumb eloquence of desire? To feast him was to lose him. Their love for each other was a great love. Their granaries were overflowing with plenitude; yet they wanted to keep the sharp famine-edge of their love undulled.

"Nor were they lean little fledglings theorizing on the threshold of Love. They were robust and realized souls. They had loved before, with others, in the days before they met; and in those days they had throttled Love with caresses, and killed him with kisses, and buried him in the pit of satiety.

"They were not cold wraiths, this man and woman. They were warm human. They had no Saxon soberness in their blood. The color of it was sunset-red. They glowed with it. Temperamentally theirs was the French joy in the flesh. They were idealists, but their idealism was Gallic. It was not tempered by the chill and sombre fluid that for the English serves as blood. There was no stoicism about them. They were Americans, descended out of the English, and yet the refraining and self-denying of the English spirit-groping were not theirs.

"They were all this that I have said, and they were made for joy, only they achieved a concept. A curse on concepts! They played with logic, and this was their logic.—But first let me tell you of a talk we had one night. It was of Gautier's Madeline de Maupin. You remember the maid? She kissed once, and once only, and kisses she would have no more. Not that she found kisses were not sweet, but that she feared with repetition they would cloy. Satiety again! She tried to play without stakes against the gods. Now this is contrary to a rule of the game the gods themselves have made. Only the rules are not posted over the table. Mortals must play in order to learn the rules.

"Well, to the logic. The man and the woman argued thus: Why kiss once only? If to kiss once were wise, was it not wiser to kiss not at all? Thus could they keep Love alive. Fasting, he would knock forever at their hearts.

"Perhaps it was out of their heredity that they achieved this unholy concept. The breed will out, and sometimes most fantastically. Thus in them did cursed Albion array herself a scheming wanton, a bold, cold-calculating, and artful hussy. After all, I do not know. But this I know: it was out of their inordinate desire for joy that they forewent joy.

"As he said (I read it long afterward in one of his letters to her): 'To hold you in my arms, close, and yet not close. To yearn for you, and never to have you, and so always to have you.' And she: 'For you to be always just beyond my reach. To be ever attaining you, and yet never attaining you, and for this to last forever, always fresh and new, and always with the first flush upon us.'

"That is not the way they said it. On my lips their love-philosophy is mangled. And who am I to delve into their soul-stuff? I am a frog, on the dank edge of a great darkness, gazing goggle-eyed at the mystery and wonder of their flaming souls.

"And they were right, as far as they went. Everything is good...as long as it is unpossessed. Satiety and possession are Death's horses; they run in span.

"'And time could only tutor us to eke
Our rapture's warmth with custom's afterglow.'

"They got that from a sonnet of Alfred Austin's. It was called 'Love's Wisdom.' It was the one kiss of Madeline de Maupin. How did it run?

"'Kiss we and part; no further can we go;
And better death than we from high to low
Should dwindle, or decline from strong to weak'

"But they were wiser. They would not kiss and part. They would not kiss at all, and thus they planned to stay at Love's topmost peak. They married. You were in England at the time. And never was there such a marriage. They kept their secret to themselves. I did not know, then. Their rapture's warmth did not cool. Their love burned with increasing brightness. Never was there anything like it. The time passed, the months, the years, and ever the flame-winged lute-player grew more resplendent.

"Everybody marvelled. They became the wonderful lovers, and they were greatly envied. Sometimes women pitied her because she was childless; it is the form the envy of such creatures takes.

"And I did not know their secret. I pondered and I marvelled. As first I had expected, subconsciously I imagine, the passing of their love. Then I became aware that it was Time that passed and Love that remained. Then I became curious. What was their secret? What were the magic fetters with which they bound Love to them? How did they hold the grace-less elf? What elixir of eternal love had they drunk together as had Tristram and Iseult of old time? And whose hand had brewed the fairy drink?

"As I say, I was curious, and I watched them. They were love-mad. They lived in an unending revel of Love. They made a pomp and ceremonial of it. They saturated themselves in the art and poetry of Love. No, they were not neurotics. They were sane and healthy, and they were artists. But they had accomplished the impossible. They had achieved deathless desire.

"And I? I saw much of them and their everlasting miracle of Love. I puzzled and wondered, and then one day—"

Carquinez broke off abruptly and asked, "Have you ever read, 'Love's Waiting Time'?"

I shook my head.

"Page wrote it—Curtis Hidden Page, I think. Well, it was that bit of verse that gave me the clew. One day, in the window-seat near the big piano—you remember how she could play? She used to laugh, sometimes, and doubt whether it was for them I came, or for the music. She called me a 'music-sot,' once, a 'sound-debauchee.' What a voice he had! When he sang I believed in immortality, my regard for the gods grew almost patronizing, and I devised ways and means whereby I surely could outwit them and their tricks.

"It was a spectacle for God, that man and woman, years married, and singing love-songs with a freshness virginal as new-born Love himself, with a ripeness and wealth of ardor that young lovers can never know. Young lovers were pale and anæmic beside that long-married pair. To see them, all fire and flame and tenderness, at a trembling distance, lavishing caresses of eye and voice with every action, through every silence—their love driving them toward each other, and they withholding like fluttering moths, each to the other a candle-flame, and revolving each about the other in the mad gyrations of an amazing orbit-flight! It seemed, in obedience to some great law of physics, more potent than gravitation and more subtle, that they must corpore-ally melt each into each there before my very eyes. Small wonder they were called the wonderful lovers.

"I have wandered. Now to the clew. One day in the window-seat I found a book of verse. It opened of itself, betraying long habit, to 'Love's Waiting Time' The page was thumbed and limp with over-handling, and there I read:—

   "'So sweet it is to stand but just apart,
   To know each other better, and to keep
   The soft, delicious sense of two that touch...

   O love, not yet!...Sweet, let us keep our love
   Wrapped round with sacred mystery awhile,
   Waiting the secret of the coming years,
   That come not yet, not yet...sometime...not
      yet...

   Oh, yet a little while our love may grow!
   When it has blossomed it will haply die.
   Feed it with lipless kisses, let it sleep,
   Bedded in dead denial yet some while...
   Oh, yet a little while, a little while.'

"I folded the book on my thumb and sat there silent and without moving for a long time. I was stunned by the clearness of vision the verse had imparted to me. It was illumination. It was like a bolt of God's lightning in the Pit. They would keep Love, the fickle sprite, the forerunner of young life—young life that is imperative to be born!

"I conned the lines over in my mind—'Not yet, sometime'—'O Love, not yet'—'Feed it with lipless kisses, let it sleep.' And I laughed aloud, ha! ha! I saw with white vision their blameless souls. They were children. They did not understand. They played with Nature's fire and bedded with a naked sword. They laughed at the gods. They would stop the cosmic sap. They had invented a system, and brought it to the gaming-table of life, and expected to win out. 'Beware!' I cried. 'The gods are behind the table. They make new rules for every system that is devised. You have no chance to win'

"But I did not so cry to them. I waited. They would learn that their system was worthless and throw it away. They would be content with whatever happiness the gods gave them and not strive to wrest more away.

"I watched. I said nothing. The months continued to come and go, and still the famine-edge of their love grew the sharper. Never did they dull it with a permitted love-clasp. They ground and whetted it on self-denial, and sharper and sharper it grew. This went on until even I doubted. Did the gods sleep? I wondered. Or were they dead? I laughed to myself. The man and the woman had made a miracle. They had outwitted God. They had shamed the flesh, and blackened the face of the good Earth Mother. They had played with her fire and not been burned. They were immune. They were themselves gods, knowing good from evil and tasting not. 'Was this the way gods came to be?' I asked myself. 'I am a frog,' I said. 'But for my mud-lidded eyes I should have been blinded by the brightness of this wonder I have witnessed. I have puffed myself up with my wisdom and passed judgment upon gods.'

"Yet even in this, my latest wisdom, I was wrong. They were not gods. They were man and woman— soft clay that sighed and thrilled, shot through with desire, thumbed with strange weaknesses which the gods have not."

Carquinez broke from his narrative to roll

another cigarette and to laugh harshly. It was not a pretty laugh; it was like the mockery of a devil, and it rose over and rode the roar of the storm that came muffled to our ears from the crashing outside world.

"I am a frog," he said apologetically. "How were they to understand? They were artists, not biologists. They knew the clay of the studio, but they did not know the clay of which they themselves were made. But this I will say—they played high. Never was there such a game before, and I doubt me if there will ever be such a game again.

"Never was lovers' ecstasy like theirs. They had not killed Love with kisses. They had quickened him with denial. And by denial they drove him on till he was all aburst with desire. And the flame-winged lute-player fanned them with his warm wings till they were all but swooning. It was the very delirium of Love, and it continued undiminished and increasing through the weeks and months.

"They longed and yearned, with all the fond pangs and sweet delicious agonies, with an intensity never felt by lovers before nor since.

"And then one day the drowsy gods ceased nodding. They aroused and looked at the man and woman who had made a mock of them. And the man and woman looked into each other's eyes one morning and knew that something was gone. It was the flame-winged one. He had fled, silently, in the night, from their anchorites' board.

"They looked into each other's eyes and knew that they did not care. Desire was dead. Do you understand? Desire was dead. And they had never kissed. Not once had they kissed. Love was gone. They would never yearn and burn again. For them there was nothing left—no more tremblings and flutterings and delicious anguishes, no more throbbing and pulsing, and sighing and song. Desire was dead. It had died in the night, on a couch cold and unattended; nor had they witnessed its passing. They learned it for the first time in each other's eyes.

"The gods may not be kind, but they are often merciful. They had twirled the little ivory ball and swept the stakes from the table. All that remained was the man and woman gazing into each other's cold eyes. And then he died. That was the mercy. Within the week Marvin Fiske was dead—you remember the accident. And in her diary, written at this time, I long afterward read Mitchell Kennerly's:—

"'There was not a single hour
We might have kissed and did not kiss.'"

"Oh, the irony of it!" I cried out.

And Carquinez, in the firelight a veritable Mephistopheles in velvet jacket, fixed me with his black eyes.

"And they won, you said? The world's judgment! I have told you, and I know. They won as you are winning, here in your hills."

"But you," I demanded hotly; "you with your orgies of sound and sense, with your mad cities and madder frolics—bethink you that you win?"

He shook his head slowly. "Because you, with your sober bucolic régime, lose, is no reason that I should win. We never win. Sometimes we think we win. That is a little pleasantry of the gods."

THE APOSTATE

Now I wake me up to work;
I pray the Lord I may not shirk.
If I should die before the night,
I pray the Lord my work's all right.

Amen.

"If you don't git up, Johnny, I won't give you a bite to eat!"

The threat had no effect on the boy. He clung stubbornly to sleep, fighting for its oblivion as the dreamer fights for his dream. The boy's hands loosely clenched themselves, and he made feeble, spasmodic blows at the air. These blows were intended for his mother, but she betrayed practised familiarity in avoiding them as she shook him roughly by the shoulder.

"Lemme 'lone!"

It was a cry that began, muffled, in the deeps of

sleep, that swiftly rushed upward, like a wail, into passionate belligerence, and that died away and sank down into an inarticulate whine. It was a bestial cry, as of a soul in torment, filled with infinite protest and pain.

But she did not mind. She was a sad-eyed, tired-faced woman, and she had grown used to this task, which she repeated every day of her life. She got a grip on the bedclothes and tried to strip them down; but the boy, ceasing his punching, clung to them desperately. In a huddle, at the foot of the bed, he still remained covered. Then she tried dragging the bedding to the floor. The boy opposed her. She braced herself. Hers was the superior weight, and the boy and bedding gave, the former instinctively following the latter in order to shelter against the chill of the room that bit into his body.

As he toppled on the edge of the bed it seemed that he must fall head-first to the floor. But consciousness fluttered up in him. He righted himself and for a moment perilously balanced. Then he struck the floor on his feet. On the instant his mother seized him by the shoulders and shook him. Again his fists struck out, this time with more force and directness. At the same time his eyes opened. She released him. He was awake.

"All right," he mumbled.

She caught up the lamp and hurried out, leaving him in darkness.

"You'll be docked," she warned back to him.

He did not mind the darkness. When he had got into his clothes, he went out into the kitchen. His tread was very heavy for so thin and light a boy. His legs dragged with their own weight, which seemed unreasonable because they were such skinny legs. He drew a broken-bottomed chair to the table.

"Johnny!" his mother called sharply.

He arose as sharply from the chair, and, without a word, went to the sink. It was a greasy, filthy sink. A smell came up from the outlet. He took no notice of it. That a sink should smell was to him part of the natural order, just as it was a part of the natural order that the soap should be grimy with dish-water and hard to lather. Nor did he try very hard to make it lather. Several splashes of the cold water from the running faucet completed the function. He did not wash his teeth. For that matter he had never seen a toothbrush, nor did he know that there existed beings in the world who were guilty of so great a foolishness as tooth washing.

"You might wash yourself wunst a day without bein' told," his mother complained.

She was holding a broken lid on the pot as she poured two cups of coffee. He made no remark, for this was a standing quarrel between them, and the one thing upon which his mother was hard as adamant. "Wunst" a day it was compulsory that he should wash his face. He dried himself on a greasy towel, damp and dirty and ragged, that left his face covered with shreds of lint.

"I wish we didn't live so far away," she said, as he sat down. "I try to do the best I can. You know that. But a dollar on the rent is such a savin', an' we've more room here. You know that."

He scarcely followed her. He had heard it all before, many times. The range of her thought was limited, and she was ever harking back to the hardship worked upon them by living so far from the mills.

"A dollar means more grub," he remarked sententiously. "I'd sooner do the walkin' an' git the grub."

He ate hurriedly, half chewing the bread and washing the unmasticated chunks down with coffee.

The hot and muddy liquid went by the name of coffee. Johnny thought it was coffee—and excellent coffee. That was one of the few of life's illusions that remained to him. He had never drunk real coffee in his life.

In addition to the bread, there was a small piece of cold pork. His mother refilled his cup with coffee. As he was finishing the bread, he began to watch if more was forthcoming. She intercepted his questioning glance.

"Now, don't be hoggish, Johnny," was her comment. "You've had your share. Your brothers an' sisters are smaller'n you."

He did not answer the rebuke. He was not much of a talker. Also, he ceased his hungry glancing for more. He was uncomplaining, with a patience that was as terrible as the school in which it had been learned. He finished his coffee, wiped his mouth on the back of his hand, and started to rise.

"Wait a second," she said hastily. "I guess the loaf kin stand you another slice—a thin un."

There was legerdemain in her actions. With all the seeming of cutting a slice from the loaf for him, she put loaf and slice back in the bread box and conveyed to him one of her own two slices. She believed she had deceived him, but he had noted her sleight-of-hand. Nevertheless, he took the bread shamelessly. He had a philosophy that his mother, what of her chronic sickliness, was not much of an eater anyway.

She saw that he was chewing the bread dry, and reached over and emptied her coffee cup into his.

"Don't set good somehow on my stomach this morning," she explained.

A distant whistle, prolonged and shrieking, brought both of them to their feet. She glanced at the tin alarm-clock on the shelf. The hands stood at half-past five. The rest of the factory world was just arousing from sleep. She drew a shawl about her shoulders, and on her head put a dingy hat, shapeless and ancient.

"We've got to run," she said, turning the wick of the lamp and blowing down the chimney.

They groped their way out and down the stairs. It was clear and cold, and Johnny shivered at the first contact with the outside air. The stars had not yet begun to pale in the sky, and the city lay in blackness. Both Johnny and his mother shuffled their feet as they walked. There was no ambition in the leg muscles to swing the feet clear of the ground.

After fifteen silent minutes, his mother turned off to the right.

"Don't be late," was her final warning from out of the dark that was swallowing her up.

He made no response, steadily keeping on his way. In the factory quarter, doors were opening everywhere, and he was soon one of a multitude that pressed onward through the dark. As he entered the factory gate the whistle blew again. He glanced at the east. Across a ragged sky-line of housetops a pale light was beginning to creep. This much he saw of the day as he turned his back upon it and joined his work gang.

He took his place in one of many long rows of machines. Before him, above a bin filled with small bobbins, were large bobbins revolving rapidly. Upon these he wound the jute-twine of the small bobbins. The work was simple. All that was required was celerity. The small bobbins were emptied so rapidly, and there were so many large bobbins that did the emptying, that there were no idle moments.

He worked mechanically. When a small bobbin

ran out, he used his left hand for a brake, stopping the large bobbin and at the same time, with thumb and forefinger, catching the flying end of twine. Also, at the same time, with his right hand, he caught up the loose twine-end of a small bobbin. These various acts with both hands were performed simultaneously and swiftly. Then there would come a flash of his hands as he looped the weaver's knot and released the bobbin. There was nothing difficult about weaver's knots. He once boasted he could tie them in his sleep. And for that matter, he sometimes did, toiling centuries long in a single night at tying an endless succession of weaver's knots.

Some of the boys shirked, wasting time and machinery by not replacing the small bobbins when they ran out. And there was an overseer to prevent this. He caught Johnny's neighbor at the trick, and boxed his ears.

"Look at Johnny there—why ain't you like him?" the overseer wrathfully demanded.

Johnny's bobbins were running full blast, but he did not thrill at the indirect praise. There had been a time...but that was long ago, very long ago. His apathetic face was expressionless as he listened to himself being held up as a shining example. He was the perfect worker. He knew that. He had been told so, often. It was a commonplace, and besides it didn't seem to mean anything to him any more. From the perfect worker he had evolved into the perfect machine. When his work went wrong, it was with him as with the machine, due to faulty material. It would have been as possible for a perfect nail-die to cut imperfect nails as for him to make a mistake.

And small wonder. There had never been a time when he had not been in intimate relationship with machines. Machinery had almost been bred into him, and at any rate he had been brought up on it. Twelve years before, there had been a small flutter of excitement in the loom room of this very mill. Johnny's mother had fainted. They stretched her out on the floor in the midst of the shrieking machines. A couple of elderly women were called from their looms. The foreman assisted. And in a few minutes there was one more soul in the loom room than had entered by the doors. It was Johnny, born with the pounding, crashing roar of the looms in his ears, drawing with his first breath the warm, moist air that was thick with flying lint. He had coughed that first day in order to rid his lungs of the lint; and for the same reason he had coughed ever since.

The boy alongside of Johnny whimpered and sniffed. The boy's face was convulsed with hatred for the overseer who kept a threatening eye on him from a distance; but every bobbin was running full. The boy yelled terrible oaths into the whirling bobbins before him; but the sound did not carry half a dozen feet, the roaring of the room holding it in and containing it like a wall.

Of all this Johnny took no notice. He had a way of accepting things. Besides, things grow monotonous by repetition, and this particular happening he had witnessed many times. It seemed to him as useless to oppose the overseer as to defy the will of a machine. Machines were made to go in certain ways and to perform certain tasks. It was the same with the overseer.

But at eleven o'clock there was excitement in the room. In an apparently occult way the excitement instantly permeated everywhere. The one-legged boy who worked on the other side of Johnny bobbed swiftly across the floor to a bin truck that stood empty. Into this he dived out of sight, crutch and all.

The superintendent of the mill was coming along, accompanied by a young man. He was well dressed and wore a starched shirt—a gentleman, in Johnny's classification of men, and also, "the Inspector."

He looked sharply at the boys as he passed along. Sometimes he stopped and asked questions. When he did so, he was compelled to shout at the top of his lungs, at which moments his face was ludicrously contorted with the strain of making himself heard. His quick eye noted the empty machine alongside of Johnny's, but he said nothing. Johnny also caught his eye, and he stopped abruptly. He caught Johnny by the arm to draw him back a step from the machine; but with an exclamation of surprise he released the arm.

"Pretty skinny," the superintendent laughed anxiously.

"Pipe stems," was the answer. "Look at those legs. The boy's got the rickets—incipient, but he's got them. If epilepsy doesn't get him in the end, it will be because tuberculosis gets him first."

Johnny listened, but did not understand. Furthermore he was not interested in future ills. There was an immediate and more serious ill that threatened him in the form of the inspector.

"Now, my boy, I want you to tell me the truth," the inspector said, or shouted, bending close to the boy's ear to make him hear. "How old are you?"

"Fourteen," Johnny lied, and he lied with the full force of his lungs. So loudly did he lie that it started him off in a dry, hacking cough that lifted the lint which had been settling in his lungs all morning.

"Looks sixteen at least," said the superintendent.

"Or sixty," snapped the inspector.

"He's always looked that way."

"How long?" asked the inspector, quickly.

"For years. Never gets a bit older."

"Or younger, I dare say. I suppose he's worked here all those years?"

"Off and on—but that was before the new law was passed," the superintendent hastened to add.

"Machine idle?" the inspector asked, pointing at the unoccupied machine beside Johnny's, in which the part-filled bobbins were flying like mad.

"Looks that way." The superintendent motioned the overseer to him and shouted in his ear and pointed at the machine. "Machine's idle," he reported back to the inspector.

They passed on, and Johnny returned to his

work, relieved in that the ill had been averted. But the one-legged boy was not so fortunate. The sharp-eyed inspector haled him out at arm's length from the bin truck. His lips were quivering, and his face had all the expression of one upon whom was fallen profound and irremediable disaster. The overseer looked astounded, as though for the first time he had laid eyes on the boy, while the superintendent's face expressed shock and displeasure.

"I know him," the inspector said. "He's twelve years old. I've had him discharged from three factories inside the year. This makes the fourth."

He turned to the one-legged boy. "You promised me, word and honor, that you'd go to school."

The one-legged boy burst into tears. "Please, Mr. Inspector, two babies died on us, and we're awful poor."

"What makes you cough that way?" the inspector demanded, as though charging him with crime.

And as in denial of guilt, the one-legged boy replied: "It ain't nothin'. I jes' caught a cold last week, Mr. Inspector, that's all."

In the end the one-legged boy went out of the room with the inspector, the latter accompanied by the anxious and protesting superintendent. After that monotony settled down again. The long morning and the longer afternoon wore away and the whistle blew for quitting time. Darkness had already fallen when Johnny passed out through the factory gate. In the interval the sun had made a golden ladder of the sky, flooded the world with its gracious warmth, and dropped down and disappeared in the west behind a ragged sky-line of housetops.

Supper was the family meal of the day—the one meal at which Johnny encountered his younger brothers and sisters. It partook of the nature of an encounter, to him, for he was very old, while they were distressingly young. He had no patience with their excessive and amazing juvenility. He did not understand it. His own childhood was too far behind him. He was like an old and irritable man, annoyed by the turbulence of their young spirits that was to him arrant silliness. He glowered silently over his food, finding compensation in the thought that they would soon have to go to work. That would take the edge off of them and make them sedate and dignified—like him. Thus it was, after the fashion of the human, that Johnny made of himself a yardstick with which to measure the universe.

The Apostate

During the meal, his mother explained in various ways and with infinite repetition that she was trying to do the best she could; so that it was with relief, the scant meal ended, that Johnny shoved back his chair and arose. He debated for a moment between bed and the front door, and finally went out the latter. He did not go far. He sat down on the stoop, his knees drawn up and his narrow shoulders drooping forward, his elbows on his knees and the palms of his hands supporting his chin.

As he sat there, he did no thinking. He was just resting. So far as his mind was concerned, it was asleep. His brothers and sisters came out, and with other children played noisily about him. An electric globe on the corner lighted their frolics. He was peevish and irritable, that they knew; but the spirit of adventure lured them into teasing him. They joined hands before him, and, keeping time with their bodies, chanted in his face weird and uncomplimentary doggerel. At first he snarled curses at them—curses he had learned from the lips of various foremen. Finding this futile, and remembering his dignity, he relapsed into clogged silence.

His brother Will, next to him in age, having just

passed his tenth birthday, was the ringleader. Johnny did not possess particularly kindly feelings toward him. His life had early been embittered by continual giving over and giving way to Will. He had a definite feeling that Will was greatly in his debt and was ungrateful about it. In his own playtime, far back in the dim past, he had been robbed of a large part of that playtime by being compelled to take care of Will. Will was a baby then, and then, as now, their mother had spent her days in the mills. To Johnny had fallen the part of little father and little mother as well.

Will seemed to show the benefit of the giving over and the giving way. He was well-built, fairly rugged, as tall as his elder brother and even heavier. It was as though the life-blood of the one had been diverted into the other's veins. And in spirits it was the same. Johnny was jaded, worn out, without resilience, while his younger brother seemed bursting and spilling over with exuberance.

The mocking chant rose louder and louder. Will leaned closer as he danced, thrusting out his tongue. Johnny's left arm shot out and caught the other around the neck. At the same time he rapped his bony fist to the other's nose. It was a pathetically bony fist, but that it was sharp to hurt was evidenced by the squeal of pain it produced. The other children were uttering frightened cries, while Johnny's sister, Jennie, had dashed into the house.

He thrust Will from him, kicked him savagely on the shins, then reached for him and slammed him face downward in the dirt. Nor did he release him till the face had been rubbed into the dirt several times. Then the mother arrived, an anæmic whirlwind of solicitude and maternal wrath.

"Why can't he leave me alone?" was Johnny's reply to her upbraiding. "Can't he see I'm tired?"

"I'm as big as you," Will raged in her arms, his face a mess of tears, dirt, and blood. "I'm as big as you now, an' I'm goin' to git bigger. Then I'll lick you—see if I don't."

"You ought to be to work, seein' how big you are," Johnny snarled. "That's what's the matter with you. You ought to be to work. An' it's up to your ma to put you to work."

"But he's too young," she protested. "He's only a little boy."

"I was younger'n him when I started to work."

Johnny's mouth was open, further to express the sense of unfairness that he felt, but the mouth closed with a snap. He turned gloomily on his heel and stalked into the house and to bed. The door of his room was open to let in warmth from the kitchen. As he undressed in the semi-darkness he could hear his mother talking with a neighbor woman who had dropped in. His mother was crying, and her speech was punctuated with spiritless sniffles.

"I can't make out what's gittin' into Johnny," he could hear her say. "He didn't used to be this way. He was a patient little angel.

"An' he *is* a good boy," she hastened to defend. "He's worked faithful, an' he did go to work too young. But it wasn't my fault. I do the best I can, I'm sure."

Prolonged sniffling from the kitchen, and Johnny murmured to himself as his eyelids closed down, "You betcher life I've worked faithful."

The next morning he was torn bodily by his mother from the grip of sleep. Then came the meagre breakfast, the tramp through the dark, and the pale glimpse of day across the housetops as he turned his back on it and went in through the factory gate. It was another day, of all the days, and all the days were alike.

And yet there had been variety in his life—at the times he changed from one job to another, or was taken sick. When he was six, he was little mother and father to Will and the other children still younger. At seven he went into the mills—winding bobbins. When he was eight, he got work in another mill. His new job was marvellously easy. All he had to do was to sit down with a little stick in his hand and guide a stream of cloth that flowed past him. This stream of cloth came out of the maw of a machine, passed over a hot roller, and went on its way elsewhere. But he sat always in the one place, beyond the reach of daylight, a gas-jet flaring over him, himself part of the mechanism.

He was very happy at that job, in spite of the moist heat, for he was still young and in possession of dreams and illusions. And wonderful dreams he dreamed as he watched the steaming cloth streaming endlessly by. But there was no exercise about the work, no call upon his mind, and he dreamed less and less, while his mind grew torpid and drowsy. Nevertheless, he earned two dollars a week, and two dollars represented the difference between acute starvation and chronic underfeeding.

But when he was nine, he lost his job. Measles was the cause of it. After he recovered, he got work in a glass factory. The pay was better, and the work demanded skill. It was piecework, and the more skilful he was, the bigger wages he earned. Here was incentive. And under this incentive he developed into a remarkable worker.

It was simple work, the tying of glass stoppers into small bottles. At his waist he carried a bundle of twine. He held the bottles between his knees so that he might work with both hands. Thus, in a sitting position and bending over his own knees, his narrow shoulders grew humped and his chest was contracted for ten hours each day. This was not good for the lungs, but he tied three hundred dozen bottles a day.

The superintendent was very proud of him, and brought visitors to look at him. In ten hours three hundred dozen bottles passed through his hands. This meant that he had attained machine-like perfection. All waste movements were eliminated. Every motion of his thin arms, every movement of a muscle in the thin fingers, was swift and accurate.

He worked at high tension, and the result was that he grew nervous. At night his muscles twitched in his sleep, and in the daytime he could not relax and rest. He remained keyed up and his muscles continued to twitch. Also he grew sallow and his lint-cough grew worse. Then pneumonia laid hold of the feeble lungs within the contracted chest, and he lost his job in the glass-works.

Now he had returned to the jute mills where he had first begun with winding bobbins. But promotion was waiting for him. He was a good worker. He would next go on the starcher, and later he would go into the loom room. There was nothing after that except increased efficiency.

The machinery ran faster than when he had first gone to work, and his mind ran slower. He no longer dreamed at all, though his earlier years had been full of dreaming. Once he had been in love. It was when he first began guiding the cloth over the hot roller, and it was with the daughter of the superintendent. She was much older than he, a young woman, and he had seen her at a distance only a paltry half-dozen times. But that made no difference. On the surface of the cloth stream that poured past him, he pictured radiant futures wherein he performed prodigies of toil, invented miraculous machines, won to the mastership of the mills, and in the end took her in his arms and kissed her soberly on the brow.

But that was all in the long ago, before he had grown too old and tired to love. Also, she had married and gone away, and his mind had gone to sleep. Yet it had been a wonderful experience, and he used often to look back upon it as other men and women look back upon the time they believed in fairies. He had never believed in fairies nor Santa Claus; but he had believed implicitly in the smiling future his imagination had wrought into the steaming cloth stream.

He had become a man very early in life. At seven, when he drew his first wages, began his adolescence. A certain feeling of independence crept up in him, and the relationship between him and his mother changed. Somehow, as an earner and breadwinner, doing his own work in the world, he was more like an equal with her. Manhood, full-blown manhood, had come when he was eleven, at which time he had gone to work on the night shift for six months. No child works on the night shift and remains a child.

There had been several great events in his life. One of these had been when his mother bought some California prunes. Two others had been the two times when she cooked custard. Those had been events. He remembered them kindly. And at that time his mother had told him of a blissful dish she would sometime make—"floating island," she had called it, "better than custard." For years he had looked forward to the day when he would sit down to the table with floating island before him, until at last he had relegated the idea of it to the limbo of unattainable ideals.

Once he found a silver quarter lying on the sidewalk. That, also, was a great event in his life, withal a tragic one. He knew his duty on the instant the silver flashed on his eyes, before even he had picked it up. At home, as usual, there was not enough to eat, and home he should have taken it as he did his wages every Saturday night. Right conduct in this case was obvious; but he never had any spending of his money, and he was suffering from candy hunger. He was ravenous for the sweets that only on red-letter days he had ever tasted in his life.

He did not attempt to deceive himself. He knew

it was sin, and deliberately he sinned when he went on a fifteen-cent candy debauch. Ten cents he saved for a future orgy; but not being accustomed to the carrying of money, he lost the ten cents. This occurred at the time when he was suffering all the torments of conscience, and it was to him an act of divine retribution. He had a frightened sense of the closeness of an awful and wrathful God. God had seen, and God had been swift to punish, denying him even the full wages of sin.

In memory he always looked back upon that event as the one great criminal deed of his life, and at the recollection his conscience always awoke and gave him another twinge. It was the one skeleton in his closet. Also, being so made and circumstanced, he looked back upon the deed with regret. He was dissatisfied with the manner in which he had spent the quarter. He could have invested it better, and, out of his later knowledge of the quickness of God, he would have beaten God out by spending the whole quarter at one fell swoop. In retrospect he spent the quarter a thousand times, and each time to better advantage.

There was one other memory of the past dim and faded, but stamped into his soul everlasting by the savage feet of his father. It was more like a nightmare than a remembered vision of a concrete thing —more like the race-memory of man that makes him fall in his sleep and that goes back to his arboreal ancestry.

This particular memory never came to Johnny broad daylight when he was wide awake. It came at night, in bed, at the moment that his consciousness was sinking down and losing itself in sleep. It always aroused him to frightened wakefulness, and for the moment, in the first sickening start, it seemed to him that he lay crosswise on the foot of the bed. In the bed were the vague forms of his father and mother. He never saw what his father looked like. He had but one impression of his father, and that was that he had savage and pitiless feet.

His earlier memories lingered with him, but he had no late memories. All days were alike. Yesterday or last year were the same as a thousand years—or a minute. Nothing ever happened. There were no events to mark the march of time. Time did not march. It stood always still. It was only the whirling machines that moved, and they moved nowhere—in spite of the fact that they moved faster.

*   *   *

When he was fourteen, he went to work on the starcher. It was a colossal event. Something had at last happened that could be remembered beyond a night's sleep or a week's pay-day. It marked an era. It was a machine Olympiad, a thing to date from. "When I went to work on the starcher," or, "after," or "before I went to work on the starcher," were sentences often on his lips.

He celebrated his sixteenth birthday by going into the loom room and taking a loom. Here was an incentive again, for it was piece-work. And he excelled, because the clay of him had been moulded by the mills into the perfect machine. At the end of three months he was running two looms, and, later, three and four.

At the end of his second year at the looms he was turning out more yards than any other weaver, and more than twice as much as some of the less skilful ones. And at home things began to prosper as he approached the full stature of his earning power. Not, however, that his increased earnings were in excess of need. The children were growing up. They ate more. And they were going to school, and

school-books cost money. And somehow, the faster
he worked, the faster climbed the prices of things.
Even the rent went up, though the house had fallen
from bad to worse disrepair.

He had grown taller; but with his increased
height he seemed leaner than ever. Also, he was
more nervous. With the nervousness increased his
peevishness and irritability. The children had
learned by many bitter lessons to fight shy of him.
His mother respected him for his earning power, but
somehow her respect was tinctured with fear.

There was no joyousness in life for him. The procession of the days he never saw. The nights he slept
away in twitching unconsciousness. The rest of the
time he worked, and his consciousness was machine
consciousness. Outside this his mind was a blank. He
had no ideals, and but one illusion; namely, that he
drank excellent coffee. He was a work-beast. He had
no mental life whatever; yet deep down in the crypts
of his mind, unknown to him, were being weighed
and sifted every hour of his toil, every movement of
his hands, every twitch of his muscles, and prepara-
tions were making for a future course of action that
would amaze him and all his little world.

It was in the late spring that he came home from work one night aware of unusual tiredness. There was a keen expectancy in the air as he sat down to the table, but he did not notice. He went through the meal in moody silence, mechanically eating what was before him. The children um'd and ah'd and made smacking noises with their mouths. But he was deaf to them.

"D'ye know what you're eatin'?" his mother demanded at last, desperately.

He looked vacantly at the dish before him, and vacantly at her.

"Floatin' island," she announced triumphantly.

"Oh," he said.

"Floating island!" the children chorussed loudly.

"Oh," he said. And after two or three mouthfuls, he added, "I guess I ain't hungry to-night."

He dropped the spoon, shoved back his chair, and arose wearily from the table.

"An' I guess I'll go to bed."

His feet dragged more heavily than usual as he crossed the kitchen floor. Undressing was a Titan's task, a monstrous futility, and he wept weakly as he crawled into bed, one shoe still on. He was aware of a rising, swelling something inside his head that made his brain thick and fuzzy. His lean fingers felt as big as his wrist, while in the ends of them was a remoteness of sensation vague and fuzzy like his brain. The small of his back ached intolerably. All his bones ached. He ached everywhere. And in his head began the shrieking, pounding, crashing, roaring of a million looms. All space was filled with flying shuttles. They darted in and out, intricately, amongst the stars. He worked a thousand looms himself, and ever they speeded up, faster and faster, and his brain unwound, faster and faster, and became the thread that fed the thousand flying shuttles.

He did not go to work next morning. He was too busy weaving colossally on the thousand looms that ran inside his head. His mother went to work, but first she sent for the doctor. It was a severe attack of la grippe, he said. Jennie served as nurse and carried out his instructions.

It was a very severe attack, and it was a week before Johnny dressed and tottered feebly across the floor. Another week, the doctor said, and he would be fit to return to work. The foreman of the loom room visited him on Sunday afternoon, the first day of his convalescence. The best weaver in the room, the foreman told his mother. His job would be held for him. He could come back to work a week from Monday.

"Why don't you thank 'im, Johnny?" his mother asked anxiously.

"He's ben that sick he ain't himself yet," she explained apologetically to the visitor.

Johnny sat hunched up and gazing steadfastly at the floor. He sat in the same position long after the foreman had gone. It was warm outdoors, and he sat on the stoop in the afternoon. Sometimes his lips moved. He seemed lost in endless calculations.

Next morning, after the day grew warm, he took his seat on the stoop. He had pencil and paper this time with which to continue his calculations, and he calculated painfully and amazingly.

"What comes after millions?" he asked at noon, when Will came home from school. "An" how d'ye work 'em?"

That afternoon finished his task. Each day, but without paper and pencil, he returned to the stoop. He was greatly absorbed in the one tree that grew across the street. He studied it for hours at a time, and was unusually interested when the wind swayed its branches and fluttered its leaves. Throughout the week he seemed lost in a great communion with himself. On Sunday, sitting on the stoop, he laughed aloud, several times, to the perturbation of his mother, who had not heard him laugh in years.

Next morning, in the early darkness, she came to his bed to rouse him. He had had his fill of sleep all week, and awoke easily. He made no struggle, nor did he attempt to hold on to the bedding when she stripped it from him. He lay quietly, and spoke quietly.

"It ain't no use, ma."

"You'll be late," she said, under the impression that he was still stupid with sleep.

"I'm awake, ma, an' I tell you it ain't no use. You might as well lemme alone. I ain't goin' to git up."

"But you'll lose your job!" she cried.

"I ain't goin' to git up," he repeated in a strange, passionless voice.

She did not go to work herself that morning. This was sickness beyond any sickness she had ever known. Fever and delirium she could understand; but this was insanity. She pulled the bedding up over him and sent Jennie for the doctor.

When that person arrived, Johnny was sleeping gently, and gently he awoke and allowed his pulse to be taken.

"Nothing the matter with him," the doctor reported. "Badly debilitated, that's all. Not much meat on his bones."

"He's always been that way," his mother volunteered.

"Now go 'way, ma, an' let me finish my snooze."

Johnny spoke sweetly and placidly, and sweetly and placidly he rolled over on his side and went to sleep.

At ten o'clock he awoke and dressed himself. He walked out into the kitchen, where he found his mother with a frightened expression on her face.

"I'm goin' away, ma," he announced, "an' I jes' want to say good-by."

She threw her apron over her head and sat down suddenly and wept. He waited patiently.

"I might a-known it," she was sobbing.

"Where?" she finally asked, removing the apron from her head and gazing up at him with a stricken face in which there was little curiosity.

"I don't know—anywhere."

As he spoke, the tree across the street appeared with dazzling brightness on his inner vision. It seemed to lurk just under his eyelids, and he could see it whenever he wished.

"An' your job?" she quavered.

"I ain't never goin' to work again."

"My God, Johnny!" she wailed, "don't say that!"

What he had said was blasphemy to her As a mother who hears her child deny God, was Johnny's mother shocked by his words.

"What's got into you, anyway?" she demanded, with a lame attempt at imperativeness.

"Figures," he answered. "Jes' figures. I've ben doin' a lot of figurin' this week, an' it's most surprisin'."

"I don't see what that's got to do with it," she sniffled.

Johnny smiled patiently, and his mother was aware of a distinct shock at the persistent absence of his peevishness and irritability.

"I'll show you," he said. "I'm plum' tired out. What makes me tired? Moves. I've ben movin' ever since I was born. I'm tired of movin', an' I ain't goin' to move any more. Remember when I worked in the glass-house? I used to do three hundred dozen a day. Now I reckon I made about ten different moves to each bottle. That's thirty-six thousan' moves a day. Ten days, three hundred an' sixty thousan' moves a day. One month, one million an' eighty thousan' moves. Chuck out the eighty thousan'—" he spoke with the complacent beneficence of a philanthropist—"chuck out the eighty thousan', that leaves a million moves a month—twelve million moves a year.

"At the looms I'm movin' twic'st as much. That makes twenty-five million moves a year, an' it seems to me I've ben a movin' that way 'most a million years.

"Now this week I ain't moved at all. I ain't made one move in hours an' hours. I tell you it was swell, jes' settin' there, hours an' hours, an' doin' nothin'. I ain't never ben happy before. I never had any time. I've ben movin' all the time. That ain't no way to be happy. An' I ain't goin' to do it any more. I'm jes' goin' to set, an' set, an' rest, an' rest, and then rest some more."

"But what's goin' to come of Will an' the children?" she asked despairingly.

"That's it, 'Will an' the children,'" he repeated.

But there was no bitterness in his voice. He had long known his mother's ambition for the younger boy, but the thought of it no longer rankled. Nothing mattered any more. Not even that.

"I know, ma, what you've ben plannin' for Will—keepin' him in school to make a book-keeper out of him. But it ain't no use, I've quit. He's got to go to work."

"An' after I have brung you up the way I have," she wept, starting to cover her head with the apron and changing her mind.

"You never brung me up," he answered with sad kindliness. "I brung myself up, ma, an' I brung up Will. He's bigger'n me, an' heavier, an' taller. When I was a kid, I reckon I didn't git enough to eat. When he come along an' was a kid, I was workin' an' earnin' grub for him too. But that's done with. Will can go to work, same as me, or he can go to hell, I don't care which. I'm tired. I'm goin' now. Ain't you goin' to say good-by?"

She made no reply. The apron had gone over her head again, and she was crying. He paused a moment in the doorway.

"I'm sure I done the best I knew how," she was sobbing.

He passed out of the house and down the street. A wan delight came into his face at the sight of the lone tree. "Jes' ain't goin' to do nothin'," he said to himself, half aloud, in a crooning tone. He glanced wistfully up at the sky, but the bright sun dazzled and blinded him.

It was a long walk he took, and he did not walk fast. It took him past the jute-mill. The muffled roar of the loom room came to his ears, and he smiled. It was a gentle, placid smile. He hated no one, not even the pounding, shrieking machines. There was no bitterness in him, nothing but an inordinate hunger for rest.

The houses and factories thinned out and the open spaces increased as he approached the country. At last the city was behind him, and he was walking down a leafy lane beside the railroad track. He did not walk like a man. He did not look like a man. He was a travesty of the human. It was a twisted and stunted and nameless piece of life that shambled like a sickly ape, arms loose-hanging, stoop-shoul- dered, narrow-chested, grotesque and terrible.

He passed by a small railroad station and lay down in the grass under a tree. All afternoon he lay there. Sometimes he dozed, with muscles that twitched in his sleep. When awake, he lay without movement, watching the birds or looking up at the sky through the branches of the tree above him. Once or twice he laughed aloud, but without relevance to anything he had seen or felt.

After twilight had gone, in the first darkness of the night, a freight train rumbled into the station. When the engine was switching cars on to the side-track, Johnny crept along the side of the train. He pulled open the side-door of an empty box-car and awkwardly and laboriously climbed in. He closed the door. The engine whistled. Johnny was lying down, and in the darkness he smiled.

A WICKED WOMAN

It was because she had broken with Billy that Loretta had come visiting to Santa Clara. Billy could not understand. His sister had reported that he had walked the floor and cried all night. Loretta had not slept all night either, while she had wept most of the night. Daisy knew this, because it was in her arms that the weeping had been done. And Daisy's husband, Captain Kitt, knew, too. The tears of Loretta, and the comforting by Daisy, had lost him some sleep.

Now Captain Kitt did not like to lose sleep. Neither did he want Loretta to marry Billy—nor anybody else. It was Captain Kitt's belief that Daisy needed the help of her younger sister in the household. But he did not say this aloud. Instead, he always insisted that Loretta was too young to think of marriage. So it was Captain Kitt's idea that Loretta should be packed off on a visit to Mrs. Hemingway. There wouldn't be any Billy there.

Before Loretta had been at Santa Clara a week, she was convinced that Captain Kitt's idea was a good one. In the first place, though Billy wouldn't believe it, she did not want to marry Billy. And in the second place, though Captain Kitt wouldn't believe it, she did not want to leave Daisy. By the time Loretta had been at Santa Clara two weeks, she was absolutely certain that she did not want to marry Billy. But she was not so sure about not wanting to leave Daisy. Not that she loved Daisy less, but that she—had doubts.

The day of Loretta's arrival, a nebulous plan began shaping itself in Mrs. Hemingway's brain. The second day she remarked to Jack Hemingway, her husband, that Loretta was so innocent a young thing that were it not for her sweet guilelessness she would be positively stupid. In proof of which, Mrs. Hemingway told her husband several things that made him chuckle. By the third day Mrs. Hemingway's plan had taken recognizable form. Then it was that she composed a letter. On the envelope she wrote: "Mr. Edward Bashford, Athenian Club, San Francisco."

"Dear Ned," the letter began. She had once been

violently loved by him for three weeks in her pre-marital days. But she had covenanted herself to Jack Hemingway, who had prior claims, and her heart as well; and Ned Bashford had philosophically not broken his heart over it. He merely added the experience to a large fund of similarly collected data out of which he manufactured philosophy. Artistically and temperamentally he was a Greek—a tired Greek. He was fond of quoting from Nietzsche, in token that he, too, had passed through the long sickness that follows upon the ardent search for truth; that he too had emerged, too experienced, too shrewd, too profound, ever again to be afflicted by the madness of youths in their love of truth. "'To worship appearance,'" he often quoted; "'to believe in forms, in tones, in words, in the whole Olympus of appearance!'" This particular excerpt he always concluded with, "'Those Greeks were superficial— *out of profundity!*'"

He was a fairly young Greek, jaded and worn. Women were faithless and unveracious, he held—at such times that he had relapses and descended to pessimism from his wonted high philosophical calm. He did not believe in the truth of women; but, faithful to his German master, he did not strip from them the airy gauzes that veiled their untruth. He was content to accept them as appearances and to make the best of it. He was superficial—*out of profundity.*

"Jack says to be sure to say to you, 'good swimming,'" Mrs. Hemingway wrote in her letter; "and also 'to bring your fishing duds along.'" Mrs. Hemingway wrote other things in the letter. She told him that at last she was prepared to exhibit to him an absolutely true, unsullied, and innocent woman. "A more guileless, immaculate bud of womanhood never blushed on the planet," was one of the several ways in which she phrased the inducement. And to her husband she said triumphantly, "If I don't marry Ned off this time—" leaving unstated the terrible alternative that she lacked either vocabulary to express or imagination to conceive.

Contrary to all her forebodings, Loretta found that she was not unhappy at Santa Clara. True, Billy wrote to her every day, but his letters were less distressing than his presence. Also, the ordeal of being away from Daisy was not so severe as she had expected. For the first time in her life she was not lost in eclipse in the blaze of Daisy's brilliant and mature personality. Under such favorable circumstances Loretta came rapidly to the front, while Mrs. Hemingway modestly and shamelessly retreated into the background.

Loretta began to discover that she was not a pale orb shining by reflection. Quite unconsciously she became a small centre of things. When she was at the piano, there was some one to turn the pages for her and to express preferences for certain songs. When she dropped her handkerchief, there was some one to pick it up. And there was some one to accompany her in ramblings and flower gatherings. Also, she learned to cast flies in still pools and below savage riffles, and how not to entangle silk lines and gut-leaders with the shrubbery.

Jack Hemingway did not care to teach beginners, and fished much by himself, or not at all, thus giving Ned Bashford ample time in which to consider Loretta as an appearance. As such, she was all that his philosophy demanded. Her blue eyes had the direct gaze of a boy, and out of his profundity he delighted in them and forbore to shudder at the duplicity his philosophy bade him to believe lurked in their depths. She had the grace of a slender flower, the fragility of color and line of fine china, in all of which he pleasured greatly, without thought of the Life Force palpitating beneath and in spite of Bernard Shaw—in whom he believed.

Loretta bourgeoned. She swiftly developed personality. She discovered a will of her own and wishes of her own that were not everlastingly entwined with the will and the wishes of Daisy. She was petted by Jack Hemingway, spoiled by Alice Hemingway, and devotedly attended by Ned Bashford. They encouraged her whims and laughed at her follies, while she developed the pretty little tyrannies that are latent in all pretty and delicate women. Her environment acted as a soporific upon her ancient desire always to live with Daisy. This desire no longer prodded her as in the days of her companionship with Billy. The more she saw of Billy, the more certain she had been that she could not live away from Daisy. The more she saw of Ned Bashford, the more she forgot her pressing need of Daisy.

Ned Bashford likewise did some forgetting. He confused superficiality with profundity, and entangled appearance with reality until he accounted them one. Loretta was different from other women. There was no masquerade about her. She was real. He said as much to Mrs. Hemingway, and more, who agreed with him and at the same time caught her husband's eyelid drooping down for the moment in an unmistakable wink.

It was at this time that Loretta received a letter from Billy that was somewhat different from his others. In the main, like all his letters, it was pathological. It was a long recital of symptoms and sufferings, his nervousness, his sleeplessness, and the state of his heart. Then followed reproaches, such as he had never made before. They were sharp enough to make her weep, and true enough to put tragedy into her face. This tragedy she carried down to the breakfast table. It made Jack and Mrs. Hemingway speculative, and it worried Ned. They glanced to him for explanation, but he shook his head.

"I'll find out to-night," Mrs. Hemingway said to her husband.

But Ned caught Loretta in the afternoon in the big living-room. She tried to turn away. He caught her hands, and she faced him with wet lashes and trembling lips. He looked at her, silently and kindly. The lashes grew wetter.

"There, there, don't cry, little one," he said soothingly.

He put his arm protectively around her shoulder. And to his shoulder, like a tired child, she turned her face. He thrilled in ways unusual for a Greek who has recovered from the long sickness.

"Oh, Ned," she sobbed on his shoulder, "if you only knew how wicked I am!"

He smiled indulgently, and breathed in a great breath freighted with the fragrance of her hair. He thought of his world-experience of women, and drew another long breath. There seemed to emanate from her the perfect sweetness of a child—"the aura of a white soul," was the way he phrased it to himself.

Then he noticed that her sobs were increasing.

"What's the matter, little one?" he asked pettingly and almost paternally. "Has Jack been bullying you? Or has your dearly beloved sister failed to write?"

She did not answer, and he felt that he really must kiss her hair, that he could not be responsible if the situation continued much longer.

"Tell me," he said gently, "and we'll see what I can do."

"I can't. You will despise me.—Oh, Ned, I am so ashamed!"

He laughed incredulously, and lightly touched her hair with his lips—so lightly that she did not know.

"Dear little one, let us forget all about it, whatever it is. I want to tell you how I love—"

She uttered a sharp cry that was all delight, and then moaned—

"Too late!"

"Too late?" he echoed in surprise.

"Oh, why did I? Why did I?" she was moaning.

He was aware of a swift chill at his heart.

"What?" he asked.

"Oh, I...he...Billy.

"I am such a wicked woman, Ned. I know you will never speak to me again."

"This—er—this Billy," he began haltingly. "He is your brother?"

"No...he...I didn't know. I was so young. I could not help it. Oh, I shall go mad! I shall go mad!"

It was then that Loretta felt his shoulder and the encircling arm become limp. He drew away from her gently, and gently he deposited her in a big chair, where she buried her face and sobbed afresh. He twisted his mustache fiercely, then drew up another chair and sat down.

"I—I do not understand," he said.

"I am so unhappy," she wailed.

"Why unhappy?"

"Because ... he ... he wants me to marry him."

His face cleared on the instant, and he placed a hand soothingly on hers.

"That should not make any girl unhappy," he remarked sagely. "Because you don't love him, is no reason—of course, you don't love him?"

Loretta shook her head and shoulders in a vigorous negative.

"What?"

Bashford wanted to make sure.

"No," she asserted explosively. "I don't love Billy! I don't want to love Billy!"

"Because you don't love him," Bashford resumed with confidence, "is no reason that you should be unhappy just because he has proposed to you."

She sobbed again, and from the midst of her sobs she cried:—

"That's the trouble. I wish I did love him. Oh, I wish I were dead!"

"Now, my dear child, you are worrying yourself over trifles." His other hand crossed over after its mate and rested on hers. "Women do it every day. Because you have changed your mind or did not know your mind, because you have—to use an unnecessarily harsh word—jilted a man—"

"Jilted!" She had raised her head and was looking at him with tear-dimmed eyes. "Oh, Ned, if that were all!"

"All?" he asked in a hollow voice, while his hands slowly retreated from hers. He was about to speak further, then remained silent.

"But I don't want to marry him," Loretta broke forth protestingly.

"Then I shouldn't," he counselled.

"But I ought to marry him."

"*Ought* to marry him?"

She nodded.

"That is a strong word."

"I know it is," she acquiesced, while she strove to control her trembling lips. Then she spoke more calmly. "I am a wicked woman, a terribly wicked woman. No one knows how wicked I am—except Billy."

There was a pause. Ned Bashford's face was grave, and he looked queerly at Loretta.

"He—Billy knows?" he asked finally.

A reluctant nod and flaming cheeks was the reply.

He debated with himself for a while, seeming, like a diver, to be preparing himself for the plunge.

"Tell me about it." He spoke very firmly. "You must tell me all of it."

"And will you—ever—forgive me?" she asked in a faint, small voice.

He hesitated, drew a long breath, and made the plunge.

"Yes," he said desperately. "I'll forgive you. Go ahead."

"There was no one to tell me," she began. "We were with each other so much. I did not know anything of the world—then."

She paused to meditate. Bashford was biting his lip impatiently.

"If I had only known—"

She paused again.

"Yes, go on," he urged.

"We were together almost every evening."

"Billy?" he demanded, with a savageness that startled her.

"Yes, of course, Billy. We were with each other so much.... If I had only known.... There was no one to tell me.... I was so young—"

Her lips parted as though to speak further, and she regarded him anxiously.

"The scoundrel!"

With the explosion Ned Bashford was on his feet, no longer a tired Greek, but a violently angry young man.

"Billy is not a scoundrel; he is a good man," Loretta defended, with a firmness that surprised Bashford.

"I suppose you'll be telling me next that it was all your fault," he said sarcastically.

She nodded.

"What?" he shouted.

"It was all my fault," she said steadily. "I should never have let him. I was to blame."

Bashford ceased from his pacing up and down, and when he spoke, his voice was resigned.

"All right," he said. "I don't blame you in the least, Loretta. And you have been very honest. But Billy is right, and you are wrong. You must get married."

"To Billy?" she asked, in a dim, far-away voice.

"Yes, to Billy. I'll see to it. Where does he live? I'll make him."

" But I don't want to marry Billy!" she cried out in alarm. "Oh, Ned, you won't do that?"

"I shall," he answered sternly. "You must. And Billy must. Do you understand?"

Loretta buried her face in the cushioned chair back, and broke into a passionate storm of sobs.

All that Bashford could make out at first, as he listened, was: "But I don't want to leave Daisy! I don't want to leave Daisy!"

He paced grimly back and forth, then stopped curiously to listen.

"How was I to know?—Boo-hoo," Loretta was crying. "He didn't tell me. Nobody else ever kissed me. I never dreamed a kiss could be so terrible… until, boo-hoo… until he wrote to me. I only got the letter this morning."

His face brightened. It seemed as though light was dawning on him.

"Is that what you're crying about?"

"N-no."

His heart sank.

"Then what are you crying about?" he asked in a hopeless voice.

"Because you said I had to marry Billy. And I don't want to marry Billy. I don't want to leave Daisy. I don't know what I want. I wish I were dead."

He nerved himself for another effort.

"Now look here, Loretta, be sensible. What is this about kisses? You haven't told me everything."

"I—I don't want to tell you everything."

She looked at him beseechingly in the silence that fell.

"Must I?" she quavered finally.

"You must," he said imperatively. "You must tell me everything."

"Well, then...must I?"

"You must."

"He...I...we..." she began flounderingly. Then blurted out, "I let him, and he kissed me."

"Go on," Bashford commanded desperately.

"That's all," she answered.

"All?" There was a vast incredulity in his voice.

"All?" In her voice was an interrogation no less vast.

"I mean—er—nothing worse?" He was overwhelmingly aware of his own awkwardness.

"Worse?" She was frankly puzzled. "As though there could be! Billy said—"

"When did he say it?" Bashford demanded abruptly.

"In his letter I got this morning. Billy said that my...our...our kisses were terrible if we didn't get married."

Bashford's head was swimming.

"What else did Billy say?" he asked.

"He said that when a woman allowed a man to kiss her, she always married him—that it was terrible if she didn't. It was the custom, he said; and I say it is a bad, wicked custom, and I don't like it. I know I'm terrible," she added defiantly, "but I can't help it."

Bashford absent-mindedly brought out a cigarette.

"Do you mind if I smoke?" he asked, as he struck a match.

Then he came to himself.

"I beg your pardon," he cried, flinging away match and cigarette. "I don't want to smoke. I didn't meant that at all. What I mean is—"

He bent over Loretta, caught her hands in his, then sat on the arm of the chair and softly put one arm around her.

"Loretta, I am a fool. I mean it. And I mean something more. I want you to be my wife."

He waited anxiously in the pause that followed.

"You might answer me," he urged.

"I will...if—"

"Yes, go on. If what?"

"If I don't have to marry Billy."

"You can't marry both of us," he almost shouted.

"And it isn't the custom...what...what Billy said?"

"No, it isn't the custom. Now, Loretta, will you marry me?"

"Don't be angry with me," she pouted demurely.

He gathered her into his arms and kissed her.

"I wish it were the custom," she said in a faint voice, from the midst of the embrace, "because then I'd have to marry you, Ned...dear...wouldn't I?"

"JUST MEAT"

He strolled to the corner and glanced up and down the intersecting street, but saw nothing save the oases of light shed by the street lamps at the successive crossings. Then he strolled back the way he had come. He was a shadow of a man, sliding noiselessly and without undue movement through the semi-darkness. Also he was very alert, like a wild animal in the jungle, keenly perceptive and receptive. The movement of another in the darkness about him would need to have been more shadowy than he to have escaped him.

In addition to the running advertisement of the state of affairs carried to him by his senses, he had a subtler perception, a *feel*, of the atmosphere around him. He knew that the house in front of which he paused for a moment, contained children. Yet by no willed effort of perception did he have this knowledge. For that matter, he was not even aware that he knew, so occult was the impression. Yet, did a moment arise in which action, in relation to that house, were imperative, he would have acted on the assumption that it contained children. He was not aware of all that he knew about the neighborhood.

In the same way, he knew not how, he knew that no danger threatened in the footfalls that came up the cross street. Before he saw the walker, he knew him for a belated pedestrian hurrying home. The walker came into view at the crossing and disappeared on up the street. The man that watched, noted a light that flared up in the window of a house on the corner, and as it died down he knew it for an expiring match. This was conscious identification of familiar phenomena, and through his mind flitted the thought, "Wanted to know what time." In another house one room was lighted. The light burned dimly and steadily, and he had the feel that it was a sick-room.

He was especially interested in a house across the street in the middle of the block. To this house he paid most attention. No matter what way he looked, nor what way he walked, his looks and his steps always returned to it. Except for an open window above the porch, there was nothing unusual about the house. Nothing came in nor out. Nothing happened. There were no lighted windows, nor had lights appeared and disappeared in any of the windows. Yet it was the central point of his consideration. He rallied to it each time after a divination of the state of the neighborhood.

Despite his feel of things, he was not confident. He was supremely conscious of the precariousness of his situation. Though unperturbed by the footfalls of the chance pedestrian, he was as keyed up and sensitive and ready to be startled as any timorous deer. He was aware of the possibility of other intelligences prowling about in the darkness—intelligences similar to his own in movement, perception, and divination.

Far down the street he caught a glimpse of something that moved. And he knew it was no late home-goer, but menace and danger. He whistled twice to the house across the street, then faded away shadow-like to the corner and around the corner. Here he paused and looked about him carefully. Reassured, he peered back around the corner and studied the object that moved and that was coming nearer. He had divined aright. It was a policeman.

The man went down the cross street to the next

corner, from the shelter of which he watched the corner he had just left. He saw the policeman pass by, going straight on up the street. He paralleled the policeman's course, and from the next corner again watched him go by; then he returned the way he had come. He whistled once to the house across the street, and after a time whistled once again. There was reassurance in the whistle, just as there had been warning in the previous double whistle.

He saw a dark bulk outline itself on the roof of the porch and slowly descend a pillar. Then it came down the steps, passed through the small iron gate, and went down the sidewalk, taking on the form of a man. He that watched kept on his own side the street and moved on abreast to the corner, where he crossed over and joined the other. He was quite small alongside the man he accosted.

"How'd you make out, Matt?" he asked.

The other grunted indistinctly, and walked on in silence a few steps.

"I reckon I landed the goods," he said.

Jim chuckled in the darkness, and waited for further information. The blocks passed by under their feet, and he grew impatient.

"Well, how about them goods?" he asked. "What kind of a haul did you make, anyway?"

"I was too busy to figger it out, but it's fat. I can tell you that much, Jim, it's fat. I don't dast to think how fat it is. Wait till we get to the room."

Jim looked at him keenly under the street lamp of the next crossing, and saw that his face was a trifle grim and that he carried his left arm peculiarly.

"What's the matter with your arm?" he demanded.

"The little cuss bit me. Hope I don't get hydrophoby. Folks gets hydrophoby from man-bite sometimes, don't they?"

"Gave you a fight, eh?" Jim asked encouragingly.

The other grunted.

"You're harder'n hell to get information from," Jim burst out irritably. "Tell us about it. You ain't goin' to lose money just a-tellin' a guy."

"I guess I choked him some," came the answer. Then, by way of explanation, "He woke up on me."

"You did it neat. I never heard a sound."

"Jim," the other said with seriousness, "it's a hangin' matter. I fixed 'm. I had to. He woke up on me. You an' me's got to do some layin' low for a spell."

Jim gave a low whistle of comprehension.

"Did you hear me whistle?" he asked suddenly.

"Sure. I was all done. I was just comin' out."

"It was a bull. But he wasn't on a little bit. Went right by an' kept a-paddin' the hoof out a sight. Then I come back an' gave you the whistle. What made you take so long after that?"

"I was waitin' to make sure," Matt explained. "I was mighty glad when I heard you whistle again. It's hard work waitin'. I just sat there an' thought an' thought...oh, all kinds of things. It's remarkable what a fellow'll think about. And then there was a darn cat that kept movin' around the house an' botherin' me with its noises."

"An' it's fat!" Jim exclaimed irrelevantly and with joy.

"I'm sure tellin' you, Jim, it's fat. I'm plum' anxious for another look at 'em."

Unconsciously the two men quickened their pace. Yet they did not relax from their caution. Twice they changed their course in order to avoid policemen, and they made very sure that they were not observed when they dived into the dark hallway of a cheap rooming house down town.

Not until they had gained their own room on the top floor, did they scratch a match. While Jim lighted a lamp, Matt locked the door and threw the bolts into place. As he turned, he noticed that his partner was waiting expectantly. Matt smiled to himself at the other's eagerness.

"Them search-lights is all right," he said, drawing forth a small pocket electric lamp and examining it. "But we got to get a new battery. It's runnin' pretty weak. I thought once or twice it'd leave me in the dark. Funny arrangements in that house. I near got lost. His room was on the left, an' that fooled me some."

"I told you it was on the left," Jim interrupted.

"You told me it was on the right," Matt went on. "I guess I know what you told me, an' there's the map you drew."

Fumbling in his vest pocket, he drew out a folded slip of paper. As he unfolded it, Jim bent over and looked.

"I did make a mistake," he confessed.

"You sure did. It got me guessin' some for a while."

"But it don't matter now," Jim cried. "Let's see what you got."

"It does matter," Matt retorted. "It matters a lot ... to me. I've got to run all the risk. I put my head in the trap while you stay on the street. You got to get on to yourself an' be more careful. All right, I'll show you."

He dipped loosely into his trousers pocket and brought out a handful of small diamonds. He spilled them out in a blazing stream on the greasy table. Jim let out a great oath.

"That's nothing," Matt said with triumphant complacence. "I ain't begun yet."

From one pocket after another he continued bringing forth the spoil. There were many diamonds wrapped in chamois skin that were larger than those in the first handful. From one pocket he brought out a handful of very small cut gems.

"Sun dust," he remarked, as he spilled them on the table in a space by themselves.

Jim examined them.

"Just the same, they retail for a couple of dollars each," he said. "Is that all?"

"Ain't it enough?" the other demanded in an aggrieved tone.

"Sure it is," Jim answered with unqualified

approval. "Better'n I expected. I wouldn't take a cent less than ten thousan' for the bunch."

"Ten thousan'," Matt sneered. "They're worth twic't that, an' I don't know anything about joolery, either. Look at that big boy!"

He picked it out from the sparkling heap and held it near to the lamp with the air of an expert, weighing and judging.

"Worth a thousan' all by its lonely," was Jim's quicker judgment.

"A thousan' your grandmother," was Matt's scornful rejoinder. "You couldn't buy it for three."

"Wake me up! I'm dreamin'!" The sparkle of the gems was in Jim's eyes, and he began sorting out the larger diamonds and examining them. "We're rich men, Matt—we'll be regular swells."

"It'll take years to get rid of 'em," was Matt's more practical thought.

"But think how we'll live! Nothin' to do but spend the money an' go on gettin' rid of 'em."

Matt's eyes were beginning to sparkle, though sombrely, as his phlegmatic nature woke up.

"I told you I didn't dast think how fat it was," he murmured in a low voice.

"What a killin'! What a killin'!" was the other's more ecstatic utterance.

"I almost forgot," Matt said, thrusting his hand into his inside coat pocket.

A string of large pearls emerged from wrappings of tissue paper and chamois skin. Jim scarcely glanced at them.

"They're worth money," he said, and returned to the diamonds.

A silence fell on the two men. Jim played with the gems, running them through his fingers, sorting them into piles, and spreading them out flat and wide. He was a slender, weazened man, nervous, irritable, high-strung, and anæmic—a typical child of the gutter, with unbeautiful twisted features, small-eyed, with face and mouth perpetually and feverishly hungry, brutish in a catlike way, stamped to the core with degeneracy.

Matt did not finger the diamonds. He sat with chin on hands and elbows on table, blinking heavily at the blazing array. He was in every way a contrast to the other. No city had bred him. He was heavy-muscled and hairy, gorilla-like in strength and aspect. For him there was no unseen world. His eyes were full and wide apart, and there seemed in them a certain bold brotherliness. They inspired confidence. But a closer inspection would have shown that his eyes were just a trifle too full, just a shade too wide apart. He exceeded, spilled over the limits of normality, and his features told lies about the man beneath.

"The bunch is worth fifty thousan'," Jim remarked suddenly.

"A hundred thousand'," Matt said.

The silence returned and endured a long time, to be broken again by Jim.

"What in hell was he doin' with 'em all at the house?—that's what I want to know. I'd a-thought he'd kept 'em in the safe down at the store."

Matt had just been considering the vision of the throttled man as he had last looked upon him in the dim light of the electric lantern; but he did not start at the mention of him.

"There's no tellin'," he answered. "He might a-ben gettin' ready to chuck his pardner. He might a-pulled out in the mornin' for parts unknown, if we hadn't happened along. I guess there's just as many thieves among honest men as there is among thieves.

You read about such things in the papers, Jim. Pardners is always knifin' each other."

A queer, nervous look came in the other's eyes. Matt did not betray that he noted it, though he said:—

"What was you thinkin' about, Jim?"

Jim was a trifle awkward for the moment.

"Nothin'," he answered. "Only I was thinkin' just how funny it was—all them jools at his house. What made you ask?"

"Nothin'. I was just wonderin', that was all."

The silence settled down, broken by an occasional low and nervous giggle on the part of Jim. He was overcome by the spread of gems. It was not that he felt their beauty. He was unaware that they were beautiful in themselves. But in them his swift imagination visioned the joys of life they would buy, and all the desires and appetites of his diseased mind and sickly flesh were tickled by the promise they extended. He builded wondrous, orgy-haunted castles out of their brilliant fires, and was appalled at what he builded. Then it was that he giggled. It was all too impossible to be real. And yet there they blazed on the table before him, fanning the flame of the lust of him, and he giggled again.

"I guess we might as well count 'em," Matt said suddenly, tearing himself away from his own visions. "You watch me an' see that it's square, because you an' me has got to be on the square, Jim. Understand?"

Jim did not like this, and betrayed it in his eyes, while Matt did not like what he saw in his partner's eyes.

"Understand?" Matt repeated, almost menacingly.

"Ain't we always ben square?" the other replied, on the defensive, what of the treachery already whispering in him.

"It don't cost nothin', bein' square in hard times," Matt retorted. "It's bein' square in prosperity that counts. When we ain't got nothin', we can't help bein' square. We're prosperous now, an' we've got to be business men—honest business men. Understand?"

"That's the talk for me," Jim approved, but deep down in the meagre soul of him,—and in spite of him,—wanton and lawless thoughts were stirring like chained beasts.

Matt stepped to the food shelf behind the two-burner kerosene cooking stove. He emptied the tea from a paper bag, and from a second bag emptied some red peppers. Returning to the table with the bags, he put into them the two sizes of small diamonds. Then he counted the large gems and wrapped them in their tissue paper and chamois skin.

"Hundred an' forty-seven good-sized ones," was his inventory; "twenty real big ones; two big boys and one whopper; an' a couple of fistfuls of teeny ones an' dust."

He looked at Jim.

"Correct," was the response.

He wrote the count out on a slip of memorandum paper, and made a copy of it, giving one slip to his partner and retaining the other.

"Just for reference," he said.

Again he had recourse to the food shelf, where he emptied the sugar from a large paper bag. Into this he thrust the diamonds, large and small, wrapped it up in a bandana handkerchief, and stowed it away under his pillow. Then he sat down on the edge of the bed and took off his shoes.

"An' you think they're worth a hundred thousan'?" Jim asked, pausing and looking up from the unlacing of his shoe.

"Sure," was the answer. "I seen a dance-house

girl down in Arizona once, with some big sparklers on her. They wasn't real. She said if they was she wouldn't be dancin'. Said they'd be worth all of fifty thousan', an' she didn't have a dozen of 'em all told."

"Who'd work for a livin'?" Jim triumphantly demanded. "Pick an' shovel work!" he sneered. "Work like a dog all my life, an' save all my wages, an' I wouldn't have half as much as we got to-night."

"Dish washin's about your measure, an' you couldn't get more'n twenty a month an' board. Your figgers is 'way off, but your point is well taken. Let them that likes it, work. I rode range for thirty a month when I was young an' foolish. Well, I'm older, an' I ain't ridin' range."

He got into bed on one side. Jim put out the light and followed him in on the other side.

"How's your arm feel?" Jim queried amiably.

Such concern was unusual, and Matt noted it, and replied:—

"I guess there's no danger of hydrophoby. What made you ask?"

Jim felt in himself a guilty stir, and under his breath he cursed the other's way of asking disagreeable questions; but aloud he answered:—

"Nothin', only you seemed scared of it at first. What are you goin' to do with your share, Matt?"

"Buy a cattle ranch in Arizona an' set down an' pay other men to ride range for me. There's some several I'd like to see askin' a job from me, damn them! An' now you shut your face, Jim. It'll be some time before I buy that ranch. Just now I'm goin' to sleep."

But Jim lay long awake, nervous and twitching, rolling about restlessly and rolling himself wide awake every time he dozed. The diamonds still blazed under his eyelids, and the fire of them hurt. Matt, in spite of his heavy nature, slept lightly, like a wild animal alert in its sleep; and Jim noticed, every time he moved, that his partner's body moved sufficiently to show that it had received the impression and that it was trembling on the verge of awakening. For that matter, Jim did not know whether or not, frequently, the other was awake. Once, quietly, betokening complete consciousness, Matt said to him: "Aw, go to sleep, Jim. Don't worry about them jools. They'll keep." And Jim had thought that at that particular moment Matt had been surely asleep.

In the late morning Matt was awake with Jim's

first movement, and thereafter he awoke and dozed with him until midday, when they got up together and began dressing.

"I'm goin' out to get a paper an' some bread," Matt said. "You boil the coffee."

As Jim listened, unconsciously his gaze left Matt's face and roved to the pillow, beneath which was the bundle wrapped in the bandana handkerchief. On the instant Matt's face became like a wild beast's.

"Look here, Jim," he snarled. "You've got to play square. If you do me dirt, I'll fix you. Understand? I'd eat you, Jim. You know that. I'd bite right into your throat an' eat you like that much beefsteak."

His sunburned skin was black with the surge of blood in it, and his tobacco-stained teeth were exposed by the snarling lips. Jim shivered and involuntarily cowered. There was death in the man he looked at. Only the night before that black-faced man had killed another with his hands, and it had not hurt his sleep. And in his own heart Jim was aware of a sneaking guilt, of a train of thought that merited all that was threatened.

Matt passed out, leaving him still shivering. Then a hatred twisted his own face, and he softly hurled savage curses at the door. He remembered the jewels, and hastened to the bed, feeling under the pillow for the bandana bundle. He crushed it with his fingers to make certain that it still contained the diamonds. Assured that Matt had not carried them away, he looked toward the kerosene stove with a guilty start. Then he hurriedly lighted it, filled the coffee-pot at the sink, and put it over the flame.

The coffee was boiling when Matt returned, and while the latter cut the bread and put a slice of butter on the table, Jim poured out the coffee. It was not until he sat down and had taken a few sips of the coffee, that Matt pulled out the morning paper from his pocket.

"We was way off," he said. "I told you I didn't dast figger out how fat it was. Look at that."

He pointed to the head-lines on the first page.

"SWIFT NEMESIS ON BUJANNOFF'S TRACK," they read. "MURDERED IN HIS SLEEP AFTER ROBBING HIS PARTNER."

"There you have it!" Matt cried. "He robbed his partner—robbed him like a dirty thief."

"Half a million of jewels missin'," Jim read aloud. He put the paper down and stared at Matt.

"That's what I told you," the latter said. "What in hell do we know about jools? Half a million!—an' the best I could figger it was a hundred thousan'. Go on an' read the rest of it."

They read on silently, their heads side by side, the untouched coffee growing cold; and ever and anon one or the other burst forth with some salient printed fact.

"I'd like to seen Metzner's face when he opened the safe at the store this mornin'," Jim gloated.

"He hit the high places right away for Bujannoff's house," Matt explained. "Go on an' read."

"Was to have sailed last night at ten on the *Sajoda* for the South Seas—steamship delayed by extra freight—"

"That's why we caught 'm in bed," Matt interrupted. "It was just luck—like pickin' a fifty-to-one winner."

"*Sajoda* sailed at six this mornin'—"

"He didn't catch her," Matt said. "I saw his alarm-clock was set at five. That'd given 'm plenty of time…only I come along an' put the *kibosh* on his time. Go on."

"Adolph Metzner in despair—the famous

Haythorne pearl necklace—magnificently assorted pearls—valued by experts at from fifty to seventy thousan' dollars."

Jim broke off to swear vilely and solemnly, concluding with, "Those damn oyster-eggs worth all that money!"

He licked his lips and added, "They was beauties an' no mistake."

"Big Brazilian gem," he read on. "Eighty thousan' dollars—many valuable gems of the first water—several thousan' small diamonds well worth forty thousan'."

"What you don't know about jools is worth knowin'," Matt smiled good-humoredly.

"Theory of the sleuths," Jim read. "Thieves must have known—cleverly kept watch on Bujannoff's actions—must have learned his plan and trailed him to his house with the fruits of his robbery—"

"Clever—hell!" Matt broke out. "That's the way reputations is made...in the noospapers. How'd we know he was robbin' his pardner?"

"Anyway, we've got the goods," Jim grinned. "Let's look at 'em again."

He assured himself that the door was locked and

bolted, while Matt brought out the bundle in the bandana and opened it on the table.

"Ain't they beauties, though!" Jim exclaimed at sight of the pearls; and for a time he had eyes only for them. "Accordin' to the experts, worth from fifty to seventy thousan' dollars."

"An' women like them things," Matt commented. "An' they'll do everything to get 'em—sell themselves, commit murder, anything."

"Just like you an' me."

"Not on your life," Matt retorted, "I'll commit murder for 'em, but not for their own sakes, but for sake of what they'll get me. That's the difference. Women want the jools for themselves, an' I want the jools for the women an' such things they'll get me."

"Lucky that men an' women don't want the same things," Jim remarked.

"That's what makes commerce," Matt agreed; "people wantin' different things."

In the middle of the afternoon Jim went out to buy food. While he was gone, Matt cleared the table of the jewels, wrapping them up as before and putting them under the pillow. Then he lighted the kerosene stove and started to boil water for the coffee. A few minutes later, Jim returned.

"Most surprising," he remarked. "Streets, an' stores, an' people just like they always was. Nothin' changed. An' me walkin' along through it all a millionnaire. Nobody looked at me an' guessed it."

Matt grunted unsympathetically. He had little comprehension of the lighter whims and fancies of his partner's imagination.

"Did you get a porterhouse?" he demanded.

"Sure, an' an inch thick. It's a peach. Look at it."

He unwrapped the steak and held it up for the other's inspection. Then he made the coffee and set the table, while Matt fried the steak.

"Don't put on too much of them red peppers," Jim warned. "I ain't used to your Mexican cookin'. You always season too hot."

Matt grunted a laugh and went on with his cooking. Jim poured out the coffee, but first, into the nicked china cup, he emptied a powder he had carried in his vest pocket wrapped in a rice-paper. He had turned his back for the moment on his partner, but he did not dare to glance around at him. Matt placed a newspaper on the table, and on the newspaper set the hot frying-pan. He cut the steak in half, and served Jim and himself.

"Eat her while she's hot," he counselled, and with knife and fork set the example.

"She's a dandy," was Jim's judgment, after his first mouthful. "But I tell you one thing straight. I'm never goin' to visit you on that Arizona ranch, so you needn't ask me."

"What's the matter now?" Matt asked.

"Hell's the matter," was the answer. "The Mexican cookin' on your ranch'd be too much for me. If I've got hell a-comin' in the next life, I'm not goin' to torment my insides in this one. Damned peppers!"

He smiled, expelled his breath forcibly to cool his burning mouth, drank some coffee, and went on eating the steak.

"What do you think about the next life anyway, Matt?" he asked a little later, while secretly he wondered why the other had not yet touched his coffee.

"Ain't no next life," Matt answered, pausing from the steak to take his first sip of coffee. "Nor heaven nor hell, nor nothin'. You get all that's comin' right here in this life."

"An' afterward?" Jim queried out of his morbid

curiosity, for he knew that he looked upon a man that was soon to die. "An' afterward?" he repeated.

"Did you ever see a man two weeks dead?" the other asked.

Jim shook his head.

"Well, I have. He was like this beefsteak you an' me is eatin'. It was once steer cavortin' over the landscape. But now it's just meat. That's all, just meat. An' that's what you an' me an' all people come to—meat."

Matt gulped down the whole cup of coffee, and refilled the cup.

"Are you scared to die?" he asked.

Jim shook his head. "What's the use? I don't die anyway. I pass on an' live again—"

"To go stealin', an' lyin' an' snivellin' through another life, an' go on that way forever an' ever an' ever?" Matt sneered.

"Maybe I'll improve," Jim suggested hopefully. "Maybe stealin' won't be necessary in the life to come."

He ceased abruptly, and stared straight before him, a frightened expression on his face.

"What's the matter?" Matt demanded.

"Nothin'. I was just wonderin'"—Jim returned to himself with an effort—"about this dyin', that was all."

But he could not shake off the fright that had startled him. It was as if an unseen thing of gloom had passed him by, casting upon him the intangible shadow of its presence. He was aware of a feeling of foreboding. Something ominous was about to happen. Calamity hovered in the air. He gazed fixedly across the table at the other man. He could not understand. Was it that he had blundered and poisoned himself? No, Matt had the nicked cup, and he had certainly put the poison in the nicked cup.

It was all his own imagination, was his next thought. It had played him tricks before. Fool! Of course it was. Of course something was about to happen, but it was about to happen to Matt. Had not Matt drunk the whole cup of coffee?

Jim brightened up and finished his steak, sopping bread in the gravy when the meat was gone.

"When I was a kid—" he began, but broke off abruptly.

Again the unseen thing of gloom had fluttered, and his being was vibrant with premonition of impending misfortune. He felt a disruptive influence at work in the flesh of him, and in all his muscles there was a seeming that they were about to begin to twitch. He sat back suddenly, and as suddenly leaned forward with his elbows on the table. A tremor ran dimly through the muscles of his body. It was like the first rustling of leaves before the oncoming of wind. He clenched his teeth. It came again, a spasmodic tensing of his muscles. He knew panic at the revolt within his being. His muscles no longer recognized his mastery over them. Again they spasmodically tensed, despite the will of him, for he had willed that they should not tense. This was revolution within himself, this was anarchy; and the terror of impotence rushed up in him as his flesh gripped and seemed to seize him in a clutch, chills running up and down his back and sweat starting on his brow. He glanced about the room, and all the details of it smote him with a strange sense of familiarity. It was as though he had just returned from a long journey. He looked across the table at his partner. Matt was watching him and smiling. An expression of horror spread over Jim's face.

"My God, Matt!" he screamed. "You ain't doped me?"

Matt smiled and continued to watch him. In the

paroxysm that followed, Jim did not become unconscious. His muscles tensed and twitched and knotted, hurting him and crushing him in their savage grip. And in the midst of it all, it came to him that Matt was acting queerly. He was travelling the same road. The smile had gone from his face, and there was on it an intent expression, as if he were listening to some inner tale of himself and trying to divine the message. Matt got up and walked across the room and back again, then sat down.

"You did this, Jim," he said quietly.

"But I didn't think you'd try to fix *me*," Jim answered reproachfully.

"Oh, I fixed you all right," Matt said, with teeth close together and shivering body. "What did you give me?"

"Strychnine."

"Same as I gave you," Matt volunteered. "It's a hell of a mess, ain't it?"

"You're lyin', Matt," Jim pleaded. "You ain't doped me, have you?"

"I sure did, Jim; an' I didn't overdose you, neither. I cooked it in as neat as you please in your half the porterhouse.—Hold on! Where're you goin'?"

Jim had made a dash for the door, and was throwing back the bolts. Matt sprang in between and shoved him away.

"Drug store," Jim panted. "Drug store."

"No you don't. You'll stay right here. There ain't goin' to be any runnin' out an' makin' a poison play on the street—not with all them jools reposin' under the pillow. Savve? Even if you didn't die, you'd be in the hands of the police with a whole lot of explanations comin'. Emetics is the stuff for poison. I'm just as bad bit as you, an' I'm goin' to take a emetic. That's all they'd give you at a drug store, anyway."

He thrust Jim back into the middle of the room and shot the bolts into place. As he went across the floor to the food shelf, he passed one hand over his brow and flung off the beaded sweat. It spattered audibly on the floor. Jim watched agonizedly as Matt got the mustard can and a cup and ran for the sink. He stirred a cupful of mustard and water and drank it down. Jim had followed him and was reaching with trembling hands for the empty cup. Again Matt shoved him away. As he mixed a second cupful, he demanded:—

"D'you think one cup'll do for me? You can wait till I'm done."

Jim started to totter toward the door, but Matt checked him.

"If you monkey with that door, I'll twist your neck. Savve? You can take yours when I'm done. An' if it saves you, I'll twist your neck, anyway. You ain't got no chance, nohow. I told you many times what you'd get if you did me dirt."

"But you did me dirt, too," Jim articulated with an effort.

Matt was drinking the second cupful, and did not answer. The sweat had got into Jim's eyes, and he could scarcely see his way to the table, where he got a cup for himself. But Matt was mixing a third cupful, and, as before, thrust him away.

"I told you to wait till I was done," Matt growled. "Get outa my way."

And Jim supported his twitching body by holding on to the sink, the while he yearned toward the yellowish concoction that stood for life. It was by sheer will that he stood and clung to the sink. His flesh strove to double him up and bring him to the floor. Matt drank the third cupful, and with difficulty managed to get to a chair and sit down. His first paroxysm was passing. The spasms that afflicted him were dying away. This good effect he ascribed to the mustard and water. He was safe, at any rate. He wiped the sweat from his face, and, in the interval of calm, found room for curiosity. He looked at his partner.

A spasm had shaken the mustard can out of Jim's hands, and the contents were spilled upon the floor. He stooped to scoop some of the mustard into the cup, and the succeeding spasm doubled him upon the floor. Matt smiled.

"Stay with it," he encouraged. "It's the stuff all right. It's fixed me up."

Jim heard him and turned toward him a stricken face, twisted with suffering and pleading. Spasm now followed spasm till he was in convulsions, rolling on the floor and yellowing his face and hair in the mustard.

Matt laughed hoarsely at the sight, but the laugh broke midway. A tremor had run through his body. A new paroxysm was beginning. He arose and staggered across to the sink, where, with probing forefinger, he vainly strove to assist the action of the emetic. In the end, he clung to the sink as Jim had clung, filled with the horror of going down to the floor.

The other's paroxysm had passed, and he sat up, weak and fainting, too weak to rise, his forehead dripping, his lips flecked with a foam made yellow by the mustard in which he had rolled. He rubbed his eyes with his knuckles, and groans that were like whines came from his throat.

"What are you snifflin' about?" Matt demanded out of his agony. "All you got to do is die. An' when you die you're dead."

"I . . . ain't . . . snifflin' . . . it's . . . the . . . mustard . . . stingin' . . . my . . . eyes," Jim panted with desperate slowness.

It was his last successful attempt at speech. Thereafter he babbled incoherently, pawing the air with shaking arms till a fresh convulsion stretched him on the floor.

Matt struggled back to the chair, and, doubled up on it, with his arms clasped about his knees, he fought with his disintegrating flesh. He came out of the convulsion cool and weak. He looked to see how it went with the other, and saw him lying motionless.

He tried to soliloquize, to be facetious, to have his last grim laugh at life, but his lips made only incoherent sounds. The thought came to him that the emetic had failed, and that nothing remained but the drug store. He looked toward the door and drew himself to his feet. There he saved himself from falling by clutching the chair. Another paroxysm had begun. And in the midst of the paroxysm, with his body and all the parts of it flying apart and writhing and twisting back again into knots, he clung to the chair and shoved it before him across the floor. The last shreds of his will were leaving him when he gained the door. He turned the key and shot back one bolt. He fumbled for the second bolt, but failed. Then he leaned his weight against the door and slid down gently to the floor.

CREATED HE THEM

She met him at the door.

"I did not think you would be so early."

"It is half past eight." He looked at his watch. "The train leaves at 9:12."

He was very businesslike, until he saw her lips tremble as she abruptly turned and led the way.

"It'll be all right, little woman," he said soothingly. "Doctor Bodineau's the man. He'll pull him through, you'll see."

They entered the living-room. His glance quested apprehensively about, then turned to her.

"Where's Al?"

She did not answer, but with a sudden impulse came close to him and stood motionless. She was a slender, dark-eyed woman, in whose face was stamped the strain and stress of living. But the fine lines and the haunted look in the eyes were not the handiwork of mere worry. He knew whose handiwork it was as he looked upon it, and she knew when she consulted her mirror.

"It's no use, Mary," he said. He put his hand on her shoulder. "We've tried everything. It's a wretched business, I know, but what else can we do? You've failed. Doctor Bodineau's all that's left."

"If I had another chance..." she began falteringly.

"We've threshed that all out," he answered harshly. "You've got to buck up, now. You know what conclusion we arrived at. You know you haven't the ghost of a hope in another chance."

She shook her head. "I know it. But it is terrible, the thought of his going away to fight it out alone."

"He won't be alone. There's Doctor Bodineau. And besides, it's a beautiful place."

She remained silent.

"It is the only thing," he said.

"It is the only thing," she repeated mechanically.

He looked at his watch. "Where's Al?"

"I'll send him."

When the door had closed behind her, he walked over to the window and looked out, drumming absently with his knuckles on the pane.

"Hello."

He turned and responded to the greeting of the man who had just entered. There was a perceptible drag to the man's feet as he walked across toward the window and paused irresolutely halfway.

"I've changed my mind, George," he announced hurriedly and nervously. "I'm not going."

He plucked at his sleeve, shuffled with his feet, dropped his eyes, and with a strong effort raised them again to confront the other.

George regarded him silently, his nostrils distending and his lean fingers unconsciously crooking like an eagle's talons about to clutch.

In line and feature there was much of resemblance between the two men; and yet, in the strongest resemblances there was a radical difference. Theirs were the same black eyes, but those of the man at the window were sharp and straight looking, while those of the man in the middle of the room were cloudy and furtive. He could not face the other's gaze, and continually and vainly struggled with himself to do so. The high cheek bones with the hollows beneath were the same, yet the texture of the hollows seemed different. The thin-lipped mouths were from the same mould, but George's lips were firm and muscular, while Al's were soft and loose—the lips of an ascetic turned voluptuary. There was also a sag at the corners. His flesh hinted of grossness, especially so in the eagle-like aquiline nose that must once have been like the other's, but that had lost the austerity the other's still retained.

Al fought for steadiness in the middle of the floor. The silence bothered him. He had a feeling that he was about to begin swaying back and forth. He moistened his lips with his tongue.

"I'm going to stay," he said desperately.

He dropped his eyes and plucked again at his sleeve.

"And you are only twenty-six years old" George said at last. "You poor, feeble old man."

"Don't be so sure of that," Al retorted, with a flash of belligerence.

"Do you remember when we swam that mile and a half across the channel?"

"Well, and what of it?" A sullen expression was creeping across Al's face.

"And do you remember when we boxed in the barn after school?"

"I could take all you gave me."

"All I gave you!" George's voice rose momentarily to a higher pitch. "You licked me four afternoons out of five. You were twice as strong as I—three times as strong. And now I'd be afraid to land on you with a sofa cushion; you'd crumple up like a last year's leaf. You'd die, you poor, miserable old man."

"You needn't abuse me just because I've changed my mind," the other protested, the hint of a whine in his voice.

His wife entered, and he looked appeal to her; but the man at the window strode suddenly up to him and burst out:—

"You don't know your own mind for two successive minutes! You haven't any mind, you spineless, crawling worm!"

"You can't make me angry." Al smiled with cunning, and glanced triumphantly at his wife. "You can't make me angry," he repeated, as though the idea were thoroughly gratifying to him. "I know your game. It's my stomach, I tell you. I can't help it. Before God, I can't! Isn't it my stomach, Mary?"

She glanced at George and spoke composedly,

though she hid a trembling hand in a fold of her skirt.

"Isn't it time?" she asked softly.

Her husband turned upon her savagely. "I'm not going to go!" he cried. "That's just what I've been telling...him. And I tell you again, all of you, I'm not going. You can't bully me."

"Why, Al, dear, you said—" she began.

"Never mind what I said!" he broke out.

"I've said something else right now, and you've heard it, and that settles it."

He walked across the room and threw himself with emphasis into a Morris chair. But the other man was swiftly upon him. The talon-like fingers gripped his shoulders, jerked him to his feet, and held him there.

"You've reached the limit, Al, and I want you to understand it. I've tried to treat you like...like my brother, but hereafter I shall treat you like the thing that you are. Do you understand?"

The anger in his voice was cold. The blaze in his eyes was cold. It was vastly more effective than any outburst, and Al cringed under it and under the clutching hand that was bruising his shoulder muscles.

"It is only because of me that you have this house, that you have the food you eat. Your position? Any other man would have been shown the door a year ago—two years ago. I have held you in it. Your salary has been charity. It has been paid out of my pocket. Mary...her dresses...that gown she has on is made over; she wears the discarded dresses of her sisters, of my wife. Charity—do you understand? Your children—they are wearing the discarded clothes of my children, of the children of my neighbors who think the clothes went to some orphan asylum. And it is an orphan asylum...or it soon will be."

He emphasized each point with an unconscious tightening of his grip on the shoulder. Al was squirming with the pain of it. The sweat was starting out on his forehead.

"Now listen well to me," his brother went on. "In three minutes you will tell me that you are going with me. If you don't, Mary and the children will be taken away from you—to-day. You needn't ever come to the office. This house will be closed to you. And in six months I shall have the pleasure of burying you. You have three minutes to make up your mind."

Al made a strangling movement, and reached up with weak fingers to the clutching hand.

"My heart...let me go...you'll be the death of me," he gasped.

The hand thrust him down forcibly into the Morris chair and released him.

The clock on the mantle ticked loudly. George glanced at it, and at Mary. She was leaning against the table, unable to conceal her trembling. He became unpleasantly aware of the feeling of his brother's fingers on his hand. Quite unconsciously he wiped the back of the hand upon his coat. The clock ticked on in the silence. It seemed to George that the room reverberated with his voice. He could hear himself still speaking.

"I'll go," came from the Morris chair.

It was a weak and shaken voice, and it was a weak and shaken man that pulled himself out of the Morris chair. He started toward the door.

"Where are you going?" George demanded.

"Suit case," came the response. "Mary'll send the trunk later. I'll be back in a minute."

The door closed after him. A moment later, struck with sudden suspicion, George was opening the door. He glanced in. His brother stood at a sideboard, in one hand a decanter, in the other hand, bottom up and to his lips, a whiskey glass.

Across the glass Al saw that he was observed. It threw him into a panic. Hastily he tried to refill the glass and get it to his lips; but glass and decanter were sent smashing to the floor. He snarled. It was like the sound of a wild beast. But the grip on his shoulder subdued and frightened him. He was being propelled toward the door.

"The suit case," he gasped. "It's there...in that room. Let me get it."

"Where's the key?" his brother asked, when he had brought it.

"It isn't locked."

The next moment the suit case was spread open, and George's hand was searching the contents. From one side it brought out a bottle of whiskey, from the other side a flask. He snapped the case shut.

"Come on," he said. "If we miss one car, we miss that train."

He went out into the hallway, leaving Al with his wife. It was like a funeral, George thought, as he waited.

His brother's overcoat caught on the knob of the front door and delayed its closing long enough for Mary's first sob to come to their ears. George's lips were very thin and compressed as he went down the steps. In one hand he carried the suit case. With the other hand he held his brother's arm.

As they neared the corner, he heard the electric car a block away, and urged his brother on. Al was breathing hard. His feet dragged and shuffled, and he held back.

"A hell of a brother *you* are," he panted.

For reply, he received a vicious jerk on his arm. It reminded him of his childhood when he was hurried along by some angry grown-up. And like a child, he had to be helped up the car step. He sank down on an outside seat, panting, sweating, overcome by the exertion. He followed George's eyes as the latter looked him up and down.

"A hell of a brother *you* are," was George's comment when he had finished the inspection.

Moisture welled into Al's eyes.

"It's my stomach," he said with self-pity.

"I don't wonder," was the retort. "Burnt out like the crater of a volcano. Fervent heat isn't a circumstance."

Thereafter they did not speak. When they arrived at the transfer point, George came to himself with a start. He smiled. With fixed gaze that did not see the houses that streamed across his field of vision, he had himself been sunk deep in self-pity. He helped his brother from the car, and looked up the intersecting street. The car they were to take was not in sight.

Al's eyes chanced upon the corner grocery and saloon across the way. At once he became restless. His hands passed beyond his control, and he yearned hungrily across the street to the door that swung open even as he looked and let in a happy pilgrim. And in that instant he saw the white-jacketed bartender against an array of glittering glass. Quite unconsciously he started to cross the street.

"Hold on." George's hand was on his arm.

"I want some whiskey," he answered.

"You've already had some."

"That was hours ago. Go on, George, let me have some. It's the last day. Don't shut off on me until we get there—God knows it will be soon enough."

George glanced desperately up the street. The car was in sight.

"There isn't time for a drink," he said.

"I don't want a drink. I want a bottle." Al's voice became wheedling, "Go on, George. It's the last, the very last."

"No." The denial was as final as George's thin lips could make it.

Al glanced at the approaching car. He sat down suddenly on the curbstone.

"What's the matter?" his brother asked, with momentary alarm.

"Nothing. I want some whiskey. It's my stomach."

"Come on now, get up."

George reached for him, but was anticipated, for his brother sprawled flat on the pavement, oblivious to the dirt and to the curious glances of the passers-by. The car was clanging its gong at the crossing, a block away.

"You'll miss it," Al grinned from the pavement. "And it will be your fault."

George's fists clenched tightly.

"For two cents I'd give you a thrashing."

"And miss the car," was the triumphant comment from the pavement.

George looked at the car. It was halfway down

the block. He looked at his watch. He debated a second longer.

"All right," he said. "I'll get it. But you get on that car. If you miss it, I'll break the bottle over your head."

He dashed across the street and into the saloon. The car came in and stopped. There were no passengers to get off. Al dragged himself up the steps and sat down. He smiled as the conductor rang the bell and the car started. The swinging door of the saloon burst open. Clutching in his hand the suit case and a pint bottle of whiskey, George started in pursuit. The conductor, his hand on the bell cord, waited to see if it would be necessary to stop. It was not. George swung lightly aboard, sat down beside his brother, and passed him the bottle.

"You might have got a quart," Al said reproachfully.

He extracted the cork with a pocket corkscrew, and elevated the bottle.

"I'm sick…my stomach," he explained in apologetic tones to the passenger who sat next to him.

On the train they sat in the smoking-car. George felt that it was imperative. Also, having successfully caught the train, his heart softened. He felt more kindly toward his brother, and accused himself of unnecessary harshness. He strove to atone by talking about their mother, and sisters, and the little affairs and interests of the family. But Al was morose, and devoted himself to the bottle. As the time passed, his mouth hung looser and looser, while the rings under his eyes seemed to puff out and all his facial muscles to relax.

"It's my stomach," he said, once, when he finished the bottle and dropped it under the seat; but the swift hardening of his brother's face did not encourage further explanations.

The conveyance that met them at the station had all the dignity and luxuriousness of a private carriage. George's eyes were keen for the ear marks of the institution to which they were going, but his apprehensions were allayed from moment to moment. As they entered the wide gateway and rolled on through the spacious grounds, he felt sure that the institutional side of the place would not jar upon his brother. It was more like a summer hotel, or, better yet, a country club. And as they swept on through the spring sunshine, the songs of birds in his ears, and in his nostrils the breath of flowers, George sighed for a week of rest in such a place, and before his eyes loomed the arid vista of summer in town and at the office. There was not room in his income for his brother and himself.

"Let us take a walk in the grounds," he suggested, after they had met Doctor Bodineau and inspected the quarters assigned to Al. "The carriage leaves for the station in half an hour, and we'll just have time."

"It's beautiful," he remarked a moment later. Under his feet was the velvet grass, the trees arched overhead, and he stood in mottled sunshine. "I wish I could stay for a month."

"I'll trade places with you," Al said quickly.

George laughed it off, but he felt a sinking of the heart.

"Look at that oak!" he cried. "And that wood-pecker! Isn't he a beauty!"

"I don't like it here," he heard his brother mutter.

George's lips tightened in preparation for the struggle, but he said:—

"I'm going to send Mary and the children off to the mountains. She needs it, and so do they. And when you're in shape, I'll send you right on to join them. Then you can take your summer vacation before you come back to the office."

"I'm not going to stay in this damned hole, for all you talk about it," Al announced abruptly.

"Yes you are, and you're going to get your health and strength back again, so that the look of you will put the color in Mary's cheeks where it used to be."

"I'm going back with you." Al's voice was firm. "I'm going to take the same train back. It's about time for that carriage, I guess."

"I haven't told you all my plans," George tried to go on, but Al cut him off.

"You might as well quit that. I don't want any of your soapy talking. You treat me like a child. I'm not a child. My mind's made up, and I'll show you how long it can stay made up. You needn't talk to me. I don't care a rap for what you're going to say."

A baleful light was in his eyes, and to his brother he seemed for all the world like a cornered rat, desperate and ready to fight. As George looked at him he remembered back to their childhood, and it came to him that at last was aroused in Al the same old stubborn strain that had enabled him, as a child, to stand against all force and persuasion.

George abandoned hope. He had lost. This creature was not human. The last fine instinct of the human had fled. It was a brute, sluggish and stolid, impossible to move—just the raw stuff of life, combative, rebellious, and indomitable. And as he contemplated his brother he felt in himself the rising up of a similar brute. He became suddenly aware that his fingers were tensing and crooking like a thug's, and he knew the desire to kill. And his reason, turned traitor at last, counselled that he should kill, that it was the only thing left for him to do.

He was aroused by a servant calling to him through the trees that the carriage was waiting. He answered. Then, looking straight before him, he discovered his brother. He had forgotten it was his brother. It had been only a thing the moment before. He began to talk, and as he talked the way became clear to him. His reason had not turned traitor. The brute in him had merely orientated his reason.

"You are no earthly good, Al," he said.

"You know that. You've made Mary's life a hell. You are a curse to your children. And you have not made life exactly a paradise for the rest of us."

"There's no use your talking," Al interjected. "I'm not going to stay here."

"That's what I'm coming to," George continued. "You don't have to stay here." (Al's face brightened, and he involuntarily made a movement, as though about to start toward the carriage.) "On the other hand, it is not necessary that you should return with me. There is another way."

George's hand went to his hip pocket and appeared with a revolver. It lay along his palm, the butt toward Al, and toward Al he extended it. At the same time, with his head, he indicated the near-by thicket.

"You can't bluff me," Al snarled.

"It is not a bluff, Al. Look at me. I mean it. And if you don't do it for yourself, I shall have to do it for you."

They faced each other, the proffered revolver still extended. Al debated for a moment, then his eyes blazed. With a quick movement he seized the revolver.

"My God! I'll do it," he said. "I'll show you what I've got in me."

George felt suddenly sick. He turned away. He

did not see his brother enter the thicket, but he heard the passage of his body through the leaves and branches.

"Good-by, Al," he called.

"Good-by," came from the thicket.

George felt the sweat upon his forehead. He began mopping his face with his handkerchief. He heard, as from a remote distance, the voice of the servant again calling to him that the carriage was waiting. The woodpecker dropped down through the mottled sunshine and lighted on the trunk of a tree a dozen feet away. George felt that it was all a dream, and yet through it all he felt supreme justification. It was the right thing to do. It was the only thing.

His whole body gave a spasmodic start, as though the revolver had been fired. It was the voice of Al, close at his back.

"Here's your gun," Al said. "I'll stay."

The servant appeared among the trees, approaching rapidly and calling anxiously. George put the weapon in his pocket and caught both his brother's hands in his own.

"God bless you, old man," he murmured;

"and"—with a final squeeze of the hands—"good luck!"

"I'm coming, " he called to the servant; and turned and ran through the trees toward the carriage.

THE CHINAGO

"The coral waxes, the palm grows, but man departs."
—Tahitian proverb

Ah Cho did not understand French. He sat in the crowded court room, very weary and bored, listening to the unceasing, explosive French that now one official and now another uttered. It was just so much gabble to Ah Cho, and he marvelled at the stupidity of the Frenchmen who took so long to find out the murderer of Chung Ga, and who did not find him at all. The five hundred coolies on the plantation knew that Ah San had done the killing, and here was Ah San not even arrested. It was true that all the coolies had agreed secretly not to testify against one another; but then, it was so simple, the Frenchmen should have been able to discover that Ah San was the man. They were very stupid, these Frenchmen.

Ah Cho had done nothing of which to be afraid.

He had had no hand in the killing. It was true he had been present at it, and Schemmer, the overseer on the plantation, had rushed into the barracks immediately afterward and caught him there, along with four or five others; but what of that? Chung Ga had been stabbed only twice. It stood to reason that five or six men could not inflict two stab wounds. At the most, if a man had struck but once, only two men could have done it.

So it was that Ah Cho reasoned, when he, along with his four companions, had lied and blocked and obfuscated in their statements to the court concerning what had taken place. They had heard the sounds of the killing, and, like Schemmer, they had run to the spot. They had got there before Schemmer—that was all. True, Schemmer had testified that, attracted by the sound of quarrelling as he chanced to pass by, he had stood for at least five minutes outside; that then, when he entered, he found the prisoners already inside; and that they had not entered just before, because he had been standing by the one door to the barracks. But what of that? Ah Cho and his four fellow-prisoners had testified that Schemmer was mistaken. In the end they would be let go. They were all confident of that. Five men could not have their heads cut off for two stab wounds. Besides, no foreign devil had seen the killing. But these Frenchmen were so stupid. In China, as Ah Cho well knew, the magistrate would order all of them to the torture and learn the truth. The truth was very easy to learn under torture. But these Frenchmen did not torture—bigger fools they! Therefore they would never find out who killed Chung Ga.

But Ah Cho did not understand everything. The English Company that owned the plantation had imported into Tahiti, at great expense, the five hundred coolies. The stockholders were clamoring for dividends, and the Company had not yet paid any; wherefore the Company did not want its costly contract laborers to start the practice of killing one another. Also, there were the French, eager and willing to impose upon the Chinagos the virtues and excellences of French law. There was nothing like setting an example once in a while; and, besides, of what use was New Caledonia except to send men to live out their days in misery and pain in payment of the penalty for being frail and human?

Ah Cho did not understand all this. He sat in the court room and waited for the baffled judgment that would set him and his comrades free to go back to the plantation and work out the terms of their contracts. This judgment would soon be rendered. Proceedings were drawing to a close. He could see that. There was no more testifying, no more gabble of tongues. The French devils were tired, too, and evidently waiting for the judgment. And as he waited he remembered back in his life to the time when he had signed the contract and set sail in the ship for Tahiti. Times had been hard in his seacoast village, and when he indentured himself to labor for five years in the South Seas at fifty cents Mexican a day, he had thought himself fortunate. There were men in his village who toiled a whole year for ten dollars Mexican, and there were women who made nets all the year round for five dollars, while in the houses of shopkeepers there were maidservants who received four dollars for a year of service. And here he was to receive fifty cents a day; for one day, only one day, he was to receive that princely sum! What if the work were hard? At the end of the five years he would return home—that was in the contract—and he would never have to work again. He would be a rich man for life, with a house of his own, a wife, and children growing up to venerate him. Yes, and back of the house he would have a small garden, a place of meditation and repose, with goldfish in a tiny lakelet, and wind bells tinkling in the several trees, and there would be a high wall all around so that his meditation and repose should be undisturbed.

Well, he had worked out three of those five years. He was already a wealthy man (in his own country), through his earnings, and only two years more intervened between the cotton plantation on Tahiti and the meditation and repose that awaited him. But just now he was losing money because of the unfortunate accident of being present at the killing of Chung Ga. He had lain three weeks in prison, and for each day of those three weeks he had lost fifty cents. But now judgment would soon be given, and he would go back to work.

Ah Cho was twenty-two years old. He was happy and good-natured, and it was easy for him to smile. While his body was slim in the Asiatic way, his face was rotund. It was round, like the moon, and it irradiated a gentle complacence and a sweet kindliness of spirit that was unusual among his countrymen. Nor did his looks belie him. He never caused trouble, never took part in wrangling. He did not gamble. His soul was not harsh enough for the soul that must belong to a gambler. He was content with little things and simple pleasures. The hush and quiet in the cool of the day after the blazing toil in the cotton field was to him an infinite satisfaction. He could sit for hours gazing at a solitary flower and philosophizing about the mysteries and riddles of being. A blue heron on a tiny crescent of sandy beach, a silvery splatter of flying fish, or a sunset of pearl and rose across the lagoon, could entrance him to all forgetfulness of the procession of wearisome days and of the heavy lash of Schemmer.

Schemmer, Karl Schemmer, was a brute, a brutish brute. But he earned his salary. He got the last particle of strength out of the five hundred slaves; for slaves they were until their term of years was up. Schemmer worked hard to extract the strength from those five hundred sweating bodies and to transmute it into bales of fluffy cotton ready for export. His dominant, iron-clad, primeval brutishness was what enabled him to effect the transmutation. Also, he was assisted by a thick leather belt, three inches wide and a yard in length, with which he always rode and which, on occasion, could come down on the naked back of a stooping coolie with a report like a pistol-shot. These reports were frequent when Schemmer rode down the furrowed field.

Once, at the beginning of the first year of contract labor, he had killed a coolie with a single blow of his fist. He had not exactly crushed the man's head like an egg-shell, but the blow had been sufficient to addle what was inside, and, after being sick for a week, the man had died. But the Chinese had not complained to the French devils that ruled over Tahiti. It was their own lookout. Schemmer was their problem. They must avoid his wrath as they avoided the venom of the centipedes that lurked in the grass or crept into the sleeping quarters on rainy nights. The Chinagos—such they were called by the indolent, brown-skinned island folk—saw to it that they did not displease Schemmer too greatly. This was equivalent to rendering up to him a full measure of efficient toil. That blow of Schemmer's fist had been worth thousands of dollars to the Company, and no trouble ever came of it to Schemmer.

The French, with no instinct for colonization, futile in their childish playgame of developing the resources of the island, were only too glad to see the English Company succeed. What matter of Schemmer and his redoubtable fist? The Chinago that died? Well, he was only a Chinago. Besides, he died of sunstroke, as the doctor's certificate attested. True, in all the history of Tahiti no one had ever died of sunstroke. But it was that, precisely that, which made the death of this Chinago unique. The doctor said as much in his report. He was very candid. Dividends must be paid, or else one more failure would be added to the long history of failure in Tahiti.

There was no understanding these white devils. Ah Cho pondered their inscrutableness as he sat in the court room waiting the judgment. There was no telling what went on at the back of their minds. He had seen a few of the white devils. They were all alike—the officers and sailors on the ship, the French officials, the several white men on the plantation, including Schemmer. Their minds all moved in mysterious ways there was no getting at. They grew angry without apparent cause, and their anger was always dangerous. They were like wild beasts at such times. They worried about little things, and on occasion could out-toil even a Chinago. They were not temperate as Chinagos were temperate; they were gluttons, eating prodigiously and drinking more prodigiously. A Chinago never knew when an act would please them or arouse a storm of wrath. A Chinago could never tell. What pleased one time, the very next time might provoke an outburst of anger. There was a curtain behind the eyes of the white devils that screened the backs of their minds from the Chinago's gaze. And then, on top of it all, was that terrible efficiency of the white devils, that ability to do things, to make things go, to work results, to bend to their wills all creeping, crawling things, and the powers of the very elements themselves. Yes, the white men were strange and wonderful, and they were devils. Look at Schemmer.

Ah Cho wondered why the judgment was so long in forming. Not a man on trial had laid hand on Chung Ga. Ah San alone had killed him. Ah San had done it, bending Chung Ga's head back with one hand by a grip of his queue, and with the other hand, from behind, reaching over and driving the knife into his body. Twice had he driven it in. There in the court room, with closed eyes, Ah Cho saw the killing acted over again—the squabble, the vile words bandied back and forth, the filth and insult flung upon venerable ancestors, the curses laid upon unbegotten generations, the leap of Ah San, the grip on the queue of Chung Ga, the knife that sank twice into his flesh, the bursting open of the door, the irruption of Schemmer, the dash for the door, the escape of Ah San, the flying belt of Schemmer that drove the rest into the corner, and the firing of the revolver as a signal that brought help to Schemmer. Ah Cho shivered as he lived it over. One blow of the belt had bruised his cheek, taking off some of the skin. Schemmer had pointed to the bruises when, on the witness-stand, he had identified Ah Cho. It was only just now that the marks had become no longer visible. That had been a blow. Half an inch nearer the centre and it would have taken out his eye. Then Ah Cho forgot the whole happening in a vision he caught of the garden of meditation and repose that would be his when he returned to his own land.

He sat with impassive face, while the magistrate rendered the judgment. Likewise were the faces of his four companions impassive. And they remained impassive when the interpreter explained that the five of them had been found guilty of the murder of Chung Ga, and that Ah Chow should have his head cut off, Ah Cho serve twenty years in prison in New Caledonia, Wong Li twelve years, and Ah Tong ten years. There was no use in getting excited about it. Even Ah Chow remained expressionless as a mummy, though it was his head that was to be cut off. The magistrate added a few words, and the interpreter explained that Ah Chow's face having been most severely bruised by Schemmer's strap had made his identification so positive that, since one man must die, he might as well be that man. Also, the fact that Ah Cho's face likewise had been severely bruised, conclusively proving his presence at the murder and his undoubted participation, had merited him the twenty years of penal servitude. And down to the ten years of Ah Tong, the proportioned reason for each sentence was explained. Let the Chinagos take the lesson to heart, the Court said finally, for they must learn that the law would be fulfilled in Tahiti though the heavens fell.

The five Chinagos were taken back to jail. They

were not shocked nor grieved. The sentences being unexpected was quite what they were accustomed to in their dealings with the white devils. From them a Chinago rarely expected more than the unexpected. The heavy punishment for a crime they had not committed was no stranger than the countless strange things that white devils did. In the weeks that followed, Ah Cho often contemplated Ah Chow with mild curiosity. His head was to be cut off by the guillotine that was being erected on the plantation. For him there would be no declining years, no gardens of tranquillity. Ah Cho philosophized and speculated about life and death. As for himself, he was not perturbed. Twenty years were merely twenty years. By that much was his garden removed from him—that was all. He was young, and the patience of Asia was in his bones. He could wait those twenty years, and by that time the heats of his blood would be assuaged and he would be better fitted for that garden of calm delight. He thought of a name for it; he would call it The Garden of the Morning Calm. He was made happy all day by the thought, and he was inspired to devise a moral maxim on the virtue of patience, which maxim proved a great comfort, especially to Wong Li and Ah Tong. Ah Chow, however, did not care for the maxim. His head was to be separated from his body in so short a time that he had no need for patience to wait for that event. He smoked well, ate well, slept well, and did not worry about the slow passage of time.

Cruchot was a gendarme. He had seen twenty years of service in the colonies, from Nigeria and Senegal to the South Seas, and those twenty years had not perceptibly brightened his dull mind. He was as slow-witted and stupid as in his peasant days in the south of France. He knew discipline and fear of authority, and from God down to the sergeant of gendarmes the only difference to him was the measure of slavish obedience which he rendered. In point of fact, the sergeant bulked bigger in his mind than God, except on Sundays when God's mouthpieces had their say. God was usually very remote, while the sergeant was ordinarily very close at hand.

Cruchot it was who received the order from the Chief Justice to the jailer commanding that functionary to deliver over to Cruchot the person of Ah Chow. Now, it happened that the Chief Justice had given a dinner the night before to the captain and officers of the French man-of-war. His hand was shaking when he wrote out the order, and his eyes were aching so dreadfully that he did not read over the order. It was only a Chinago's life he was signing away, anyway. So he did not notice that he had omitted the final letter in Ah Chow's name. The order read "Ah Cho," and, when Cruchot presented the order, the jailer turned over to him the person of Ah Cho. Cruchot took that person beside him on the seat of a wagon, behind two mules, and drove away.

Ah Cho was glad to be out in the sunshine. He sat beside the gendarme and beamed. He beamed more ardently than ever when he noted the mules headed south toward Atimaono. Undoubtedly Schemmer had sent for him to be brought back. Schemmer wanted him to work. Very well, he would work well. Schemmer would never have cause to complain. It was a hot day. There had been a stoppage of the trades. The mules sweated, Cruchot sweated, and Ah Cho sweated. But it was Ah Cho that bore the heat with the least concern. He had toiled three years under that sun on the plantation. He beamed and beamed with such genial good nature that even Cruchot's heavy mind was stirred to wonderment.

"You are very funny," he said at last.

Ah Cho nodded and beamed more ardently. Unlike the magistrate, Cruchot spoke to him in the Kanaka tongue, and this, like all Chinagos and all foreign devils, Ah Cho understood.

"You laugh too much," Cruchot chided. "One's heart should be full of tears on a day like this."

"I am glad to get out of the jail."

"Is that all?" The gendarme shrugged his shoulders.

"Is it not enough?" was the retort.

"Then you are not glad to have your head cut off?"

Ah Cho looked at him in abrupt perplexity and said:—

"Why, I am going back to Atimaono to work on the plantation for Schemmer. Are you not taking me to Atimaono?"

Cruchot stroked his long mustaches reflectively. "Well, well," he said finally, with a flick of the whip at the off mule, "so you don't know?"

"Know what?" Ah Cho was beginning to feel a

vague alarm. "Won't Schemmer let me work for him any more?"

"Not after to-day." Cruchot laughed heartily. It was a good joke. "You see, you won't be able to work after to-day. A man with his head off can't work, eh?" He poked the Chinago in the ribs, and chuckled.

Ah Cho maintained silence while the mules trotted a hot mile. Then he spoke: "Is Schemmer going to cut off my head?"

Cruchot grinned as he nodded.

"It is a mistake," said Ah Cho, gravely. "I am not the Chinago that is to have his head cut off. I am Ah Cho. The honorable judge has determined that I am to stop twenty years in New Caledonia."

The gendarme laughed. It was a good joke, this funny Chinago trying to cheat the guillotine. The mules trotted through a cocoanut grove and for half a mile beside the sparkling sea before Ah Cho spoke again.

"I tell you I am not Ah Chow. The honorable judge did not say that my head was to go off."

"Don't be afraid," said Cruchot, with the philan-thropic intention of making it easier for his prisoner.

"It is not difficult to die that way." He snapped his fingers. "It is quick—like that. It is not like hanging on the end of a rope and kicking and making faces for five minutes. It is like killing a chicken with a hatchet. You cut its head off, that is all. And it is the same with a man. Pouf!—it is over. It doesn't hurt. You don't even think it hurts. You don't think. Your head is gone, so you cannot think. It is very good. That is the way I want to die—quick, ah, quick. You are lucky to die that way. You might get the leprosy and fall to pieces slowly, a finger at a time, and now and again a thumb, also the toes. I knew a man who was burned by hot water. It took him two days to die. You could hear him yelling a kilometre away. But you? Ah! so easy! Chck!—the knife cuts your neck like that. It is finished. The knife may even tickle. Who can say? Nobody who died that way ever came back to say."

He considered this last an excruciating joke, and permitted himself to be convulsed with laughter for half a minute. Part of his mirth was assumed, but he considered it his humane duty to cheer up the Chinago.

"But I tell you I am Ah Cho," the other persisted. "I don't want my head cut off."

Cruchot scowled. The Chinago was carrying the foolishness too far.

"I am not Ah Chow—" Ah Cho began.

"That will do," the gendarme interrupted. He puffed up his cheeks and strove to appear fierce.

"I tell you I am not—" Ah Cho began again.

"Shut up!" bawled Cruchot.

After that they rode along in silence. It was twenty miles from Papeete to Atimaono, and over half the distance was covered by the time the Chinago again ventured into speech.

"I saw you in the court room, when the honorable judge sought after our guilt," he began. "Very good. And do you remember that Ah Chow, whose head is to be cut off—do you remember that he—Ah Chow—was a tall man? Look at me."

He stood up suddenly, and Cruchot saw that he was a short man. And just as suddenly Cruchot caught a glimpse of a memory picture of Ah Chow, and in that picture Ah Chow was tall. To the gendarme all Chinagos looked alike. One face was like another. But between tallness and shortness he could differentiate, and he knew that he had the wrong man beside him on the seat. He pulled up the mules abruptly, so that the pole shot ahead of them, elevating their collars.

"You see, it was a mistake," said Ah Cho, smiling pleasantly.

But Cruchot was thinking. Already he regretted that he had stopped the wagon. He was unaware of the error of the Chief Justice, and he had no way of working it out; but he did know that he had been given this Chinago to take to Atimaono and that it was his duty to take him to Atimaono. What if he was the wrong man and they cut his head off? It was only a Chinago when all was said, and what was a Chinago, anyway? Besides, it might not be a mistake. He did not know what went on in the minds of his superiors. They knew their business best. Who was he to do their thinking for them? Once, in the long ago, he had attempted to think for them, and the sergeant had said: "Cruchot, you are a fool! The quicker you know that, the better you will get on. You are not to think; you are to obey and leave thinking to your betters." He smarted under the recollection. Also, if he turned back to Papeete, he would delay the execution at Atimaono, and if he were wrong in turning back, he would get a reprimand from the sergeant who was waiting for the prisoner. And, furthermore, he would get a reprimand at Papeete as well.

He touched the mules with the whip and drove on. He looked at his watch. He would be half an hour late as it was, and the sergeant was bound to be angry. He put the mules into a faster trot. The more Ah Cho persisted in explaining the mistake, the more stubborn Cruchot became. The knowledge that he had the wrong man did not make his temper better. The knowledge that it was through no mistake of his confirmed him in the belief that the wrong he was doing was the right. And, rather than incur the displeasure of the sergeant, he would willingly have assisted a dozen wrong Chinagos to their doom.

As for Ah Cho, after the gendarme had struck him over the head with the butt of the whip and commanded him in a loud voice to shut up, there remained nothing for him to do but to shut up. The long ride continued in silence. Ah Cho pondered the strange ways of the foreign devils. There was no explaining them. What they were doing with him was of a piece with everything they did. First they found guilty five innocent men, and next they cut off the head of the man that even they, in their benighted ignorance, had deemed meritorious of no more than twenty years' imprisonment. And there was nothing he could do. He could only sit idly and take what these lords of life measured out to him. Once, he got in a panic, and the sweat upon his body turned cold; but he fought his way out of it. He endeavored to resign himself to his fate by remembering and repeating certain passages from the "Yin Chih Wen" ("The Tract of the Quiet Way"); but, instead, he kept seeing his dream-garden of meditation and repose. This bothered him, until he abandoned himself to the dream and sat in his garden listening to the tinkling of the wind-bells in the several trees. And lo! sitting thus, in the dream, he was able to remember and repeat the passages from "The Tract of the Quiet Way."

So the time passed nicely until Atimaono was reached and the mules trotted up to the foot of the scaffold, in the shade of which stood the impatient sergeant. Ah Cho was hurried up the ladder of the scaffold. Beneath him on one side he saw assembled all the coolies of the plantation. Schemmer had decided that the event would be a good object-lesson, and so had called in the coolies from the fields and compelled them to be present. As they caught sight of Ah Cho they gabbled among themselves in low voices. They saw the mistake; but they kept it to themselves. The inexplicable white devils had doubtlessly changed their minds. Instead of taking the life of one innocent man, they were taking the life of another innocent man. Ah Chow or Ah Cho—what did it matter which? They could never understand the white dogs any more than could the white dogs understand them. Ah Cho was going to have his head cut off, but they, when their two remaining years of servitude were up, were going back to China.

Schemmer had made the guillotine himself. He was a handy man, and though he had never seen a guillotine, the French officials had explained the principle to him. It was on his suggestion that they had ordered the execution to take place at Atimaono instead of at Papeete. The scene of the crime, Schemmer had argued, was the best possible place for the punishment, and, in addition, it would have a salutary influence upon the half-thousand Chinagos on the plantation. Schemmer had also volunteered to act as executioner, and in that capacity he was now on the scaffold, experimenting with the instrument he had made. A banana tree, of the size and consistency of a man's neck, lay under the guillotine. Ah Cho watched with fascinated eyes. The German, turning a small crank, hoisted the blade to the top of the little derrick he had rigged. A jerk on a stout piece of cord loosed the blade and it dropped with a flash, neatly severing the banana trunk.

"How does it work?" The sergeant, coming out on top the scaffold, had asked the question.

"Beautifully," was Schemmer's exultant answer. "Let me show you."

Again he turned the crank that hoisted the blade, jerked the cord, and sent the blade crashing down on the soft tree. But this time it went no more than two-thirds of the way through.

The sergeant scowled. "That will not serve," he said.

Schemmer wiped the sweat from his forehead. "What it needs is more weight," he announced. Walking up to the edge of the scaffold, he called his orders to the blacksmith for a twenty-five-pound piece of iron. As he stooped over to attach the iron to the broad top of the blade, Ah Cho glanced at the sergeant and saw his opportunity.

"The honorable judge said that Ah Chow was to have his head cut off," he began.

The sergeant nodded impatiently. He was thinking of the fifteen-mile ride before him that afternoon, to the windward side of the island, and of Berthe, the pretty half-caste daughter of Lafière, the pearl-trader, who was waiting for him at the end of it.

"Well, I am not Ah Chow. I am Ah Cho. The honorable jailer has made a mistake. Ah Chow is a tall man, and you see I am short."

The sergeant looked at him hastily and saw the mistake. "Schemmer!" he called, imperatively. "Come here."

The German grunted, but remained bent over his task till the chunk of iron was lashed to his satisfaction. "Is your Chinago ready?" he demanded.

"Look at him," was the answer. "Is he the Chinago?"

Schemmer was surprised. He swore tersely for a few seconds, and looked regretfully across at the thing he had made with his own hands and which he was eager to see work. "Look here," he said finally, "we can't postpone this affair. I've lost three hours' work already out of those five hundred Chinagos. I can't afford to lose it all over again for the right man. Let's put the performance through just the same. It is only a Chinago."

The sergeant remembered the long ride before him, and the pearl-trader's daughter, and debated with himself.

"They will blame it on Cruchot—if it is discovered," the German urged. "But there's little chance of its being discovered. Ah Chow won't give it away, at any rate."

"The blame won't lie with Cruchot, anyway," the sergeant said. "It must have been the jailer's mistake."

"Then let's go on with it. They can't blame us. Who can tell one Chinago from another? We can say that we merely carried out instructions with the Chinago that was turned over to us. Besides, I really can't take all those coolies a second time away from their labor."

They spoke in French, and Ah Cho, who did not understand a word of it, nevertheless knew that they were determining his destiny. He knew, also, that the decision rested with the sergeant, and he hung upon that official's lips.

"All right," announced the sergeant, "Go ahead with it. He is only a Chinago."

"I'm going to try it once more, just to make sure." Schemmer moved the banana trunk forward under the knife, which he had hoisted to the top of the derrick.

Ah Cho tried to remember maxims from "The Tract of the Quiet Way." "Live in concord," came to him; but it was not applicable. He was not going to live. He was about to die. No, that would not do. "Forgive malice"—yes, but there was no malice to forgive. Schemmer and the rest were doing this thing without malice. It was to them merely a piece of work that had to be done, just as clearing the jungle, ditching the water, and planting cotton were pieces of work that had to be done. Schemmer jerked the cord and Ah Cho forgot "The Tract of the Quiet Way." The knife shot down with a thud making a clean slice of the tree.

"Beautiful!" exclaimed the sergeant, pausing in the act of lighting a cigarette. "Beautiful, my friend."

Schemmer was pleased at the praise.

"Come on, Ah Chow," he said, in the Tahitian tongue.

"But I am not Ah Chow—" Ah Cho began.

"Shut up!" was the answer. "If you open your mouth again, I'll break your head."

The overseer threatened him with a clenched fist, and he remained silent. What was the good of protesting? Those foreign devils always had their way. He allowed himself to be lashed to the vertical board that was the size of his body. Schemmer drew the buckles tight—so tight that the straps cut into his flesh and hurt. But he did not complain. The hurt would not last long. He felt the board tilting over in the air toward the horizontal, and closed his eyes. And in that moment he caught a last glimpse of his garden of meditation and repose. It seemed to him that he sat in the garden. A cool wind was blowing, and the bells in the several trees were tinkling softly. Also, birds were making sleepy noises, and from beyond the high wall came the subdued sound of village life.

Then he was aware that the board had come to rest, and from muscular pressures and tensions he knew that he was lying on his back. He opened his eyes. Straight above him he saw the suspended knife blazing in the sunshine. He saw the weight which had been added, and noted that one of Schemmer's knots had slipped. Then he heard the sergeant's voice in sharp command. Ah Cho closed his eyes hastily. He did not want to see that knife descend. But he felt it—for one great fleeting instant. And in that instant he remembered Cruchot and what Cruchot had said. But Cruchot was wrong. The knife did not tickle. That much he knew before he ceased to know.

MAKE WESTING

Whatever you do, make westing! make westing!
            —Sailing directions for Cape Horn

For seven weeks the *Mary Rogers* had been between 50° south in the Atlantic and 50° south in the Pacific, which meant that for seven weeks she had been struggling to round Cape Horn. For seven weeks she had been either in dirt, or close to dirt, save once, and then, following upon six days of excessive dirt, which she had ridden out under the shelter of the redoubtable Terra Del Fuego coast, she had almost gone ashore during a heavy swell in the dead calm that had suddenly fallen. For seven weeks she had wrestled with the Cape Horn graybeards, and in return been buffeted and smashed by them. She was a wooden ship, and her ceaseless straining had opened her seams, so that twice a day the watch took its turn at the pumps.

The *Mary Rogers* was strained, the crew was

strained, and big Dan Cullen, master, was likewise strained. Perhaps he was strained most of all, for upon him rested the responsibility of that titanic struggle. He slept most of the time in his clothes, though he rarely slept. He haunted the deck at night, a great, burly, robust ghost, black with the sunburn of thirty years of sea and hairy as an orang-utan. He, in turn, was haunted by one thought of action, a sailing direction for the Horn: *Whatever you do, make westing! make westing!* It was an obsession. He thought of nothing else, except, at times, to blaspheme God for sending such bitter weather.

Make westing! He hugged the Horn, and a dozen times lay hove to with the iron Cape bearing east-by-north, or north-north-east, a score of miles away. And each time the eternal west wind smote him back and he made easting. He fought gale after gale, south to 64°, inside the antarctic drift-ice, and pledged his immortal soul to the Powers of Darkness for a bit of westing, for a slant to take him around. And he made easting. In despair, he had tried to make the passage through the Straits of Le Maire. Halfway through, the wind hauled to the north'ard of northwest, the glass dropped to 28.88, and he turned and ran before a gale of cyclonic fury, missing, by a hair's-breadth, piling up the *Mary Rogers* on the black-toothed rocks. Twice he had made west to the Diego Ramirez Rocks, one of the times saved between two snow-squalls by sighting the gravestones of ships a quarter of a mile dead ahead.

Blow! Captain Dan Cullen instanced all his thirty years at sea to prove that never had it blown so before. The *Mary Rogers* was hove to at the time he gave the evidence, and, to clinch it, inside half an hour the *Mary Rogers* was hove down to the hatches. Her new maintopsail and brand new spencer were blown away like tissue paper; and five sails, furled and fast under double gaskets, were blown loose and stripped from the yards. And before morning the *Mary Rogers* was hove down twice again, and holes were knocked in her bulwarks to ease her decks from the weight of ocean that pressed her down.

On an average of once a week Captain Dan Cullen caught glimpses of the sun. Once, for ten minutes, the sun shone at midday, and ten minutes afterward a new gale was piping up, both watches were shortening sail, and all was buried in the obscurity of a driving snow-squall. For a fortnight, once,

Captain Dan Cullen was without a meridian or a chronometer sight. Rarely did he know his position within half of a degree, except when in sight of land; for sun and stars remained hidden behind the sky, and it was so gloomy that even at the best the horizons were poor for accurate observations. A gray gloom shrouded the world. The clouds were gray; the great driving seas were leaden gray; the smoking crests were a gray churning; even the occasional albatrosses were gray, while the snow-flurries were not white, but gray, under the sombre pall of the heavens.

Life on board the *Mary Rogers* was gray,—gray and gloomy. The faces of the sailors were blue-gray; they were afflicted with sea-cuts and sea-boils, and suffered exquisitely. They were shadows of men. For seven weeks, in the forecastle or on deck, they had not known what it was to be dry. They had forgotten what it was to sleep out a watch, and all watches it was, "All hands on deck!" They caught snatches of agonized sleep, and they slept in their oilskins ready for the everlasting call. So weak and worn were they that it took both watches to do the work of one. That was why both watches were on deck so much of the time. And no shadow of a man could shirk duty. Nothing less than a broken leg could enable a man to knock off work; and there were two such, who had been mauled and pulped by the seas that broke aboard.

One other man who was the shadow of a man was George Dorety. He was the only passenger on board, a friend of the firm, and he had elected to make the voyage for his health. But seven weeks of Cape Horn had not bettered his health. He gasped and panted in his bunk through the long, heaving nights; and when on deck he was so bundled up for warmth that he resembled a peripatetic old-clothes shop. At midday, eating at the cabin table in a gloom so deep that the swinging sea-lamps burned always, he looked as blue-gray as the sickest, saddest man for'ard. Nor did gazing across the table at Captain Dan Cullen have any cheering effect upon him. Captain Cullen chewed and scowled and kept silent. The scowls were for God, and with every chew he reiterated the sole thought of his existence, which was *make westing*. He was a big, hairy brute, and the sight of him was not stimulating to the other's appetite. He looked upon George Dorety as a Jonah, and told him so, once each meal, savagely transferring the scowl from God to the passenger and back again.

Nor did the mate prove a first aid to a languid appetite. Joshua Higgins by name, a seaman by profession and pull, but a pot-wolloper by capacity, he was a loose-jointed, sniffling creature, heartless and selfish and cowardly, without a soul, in fear of his life of Dan Cullen, and a bully over the sailors, who knew that behind the mate was Captain Cullen, the lawgiver and compeller, the driver and the destroyer, the incarnation of a dozen bucko mates. In that wild weather at the southern end of the earth, Joshua Higgins ceased washing. His grimy face usually robbed George Dorety of what little appetite he managed to accumulate. Ordinarily this lavatarial dereliction would have caught Captain Cullen's eye and vocabulary, but in the present his mind was filled with making westing, to the exclusion of all other things not contributory thereto. Whether the mate's face was clean or dirty had no bearing upon westing. Later on, when 50° south in the Pacific had been reached, Joshua Higgins would wash his face very abruptly. In the meantime, at the cabin table, where gray twilight alternated with lamplight while the lamps were being filled, George Dorety sat between the two men, one a tiger and the other a hyena, and wondered why God had made them. The second mate, Matthew Turner, was a true sailor and a man, but George Dorety did not have the solace of his company, for he ate by himself, solitary, when they had finished.

On Saturday morning, July 24, George Dorety awoke to a feeling of life and headlong movement. On deck he found the *Mary Rogers* running off before a howling southeaster. Nothing was set but the lower topsails and the foresail. It was all she could stand, yet she was making fourteen knots, as Mr. Turner shouted in Dorety's ear when he came on deck. And it was all westing. She was going around the Horn at last...if the wind held. Mr. Turner looked happy. The end of the struggle was in sight. But Captain Cullen did not look happy. He scowled at Dorety in passing. Captain Cullen did not want God to know that he was pleased with that wind. He had a conception of a malicious God, and believed in his secret soul that if God knew it was a desirable wind, God would promptly efface it and send a snorter from the west. So he walked softly before God, smothering his joy down under scowls and muttered curses, and, so, fooling God, for God was the only thing in the universe of which Dan Cullen was afraid.

All Saturday and Saturday night the *Mary Rogers* raced her westing. Persistently she logged her fourteen knots, so that by Sunday morning she had covered three hundred and fifty miles. If the wind held, she would make around. If it failed, and the snorter came from anywhere between southwest and north, back the *Mary Rogers* would be hurled and be no better off than she had been seven weeks before. And on Sunday morning the wind *was* failing. The big sea was going down and running smooth. Both watches were on deck setting sail after sail as fast as the ship could stand it. And now Captain Cullen went around brazenly before God, smoking a big cigar, smiling jubilantly, as if the failing wind delighted him, while down underneath he was raging against God for taking the life out of the blessed wind. *Make westing!* So he would, if God would only leave him alone. Secretly, he pledged himself anew to the Powers of Darkness, if they would let him make westing. He pledged himself so easily because he did not believe in the Powers of Darkness. He really believed only in God though he did not know it. And in his inverted theology God was really the Prince of Darkness. Captain Cullen was a devil-worshipper, but he called the devil by another name, that was all.

At midday, after calling eight bells, Captain Cullen ordered the royals on. The men went aloft faster than they had gone in weeks. Not alone were they nimble because of the westing, but a benignant sun was shining down and limbering their stiff bodies. George Dorety stood aft, near Captain Cullen, less bundled in clothes than usual, soaking in the grateful warmth as he watched the scene. Swiftly and abruptly the incident occurred. There was a cry from the foreroyal-yard of "Man overboard!" Somebody threw a life buoy over the side, and at the same instant the second mate's voice came aft, ringing and peremptory:—

"Hard down your helm!"

The man at the wheel never moved a spoke. He knew better, for Captain Dan Cullen was standing alongside of him. He wanted to move a spoke, to move all the spokes, to grind the wheel down, hard down for his comrade drowning in the sea. He glanced at Captain Dan Cullen, and Captain Dan Cullen gave no sign.

"Down! Hard down!" the second mate roared, as he sprang aft.

But he ceased springing and commanding, and stood still, when he saw Dan Cullen by the wheel. And big Dan Cullen puffed at his cigar and said nothing. Astern, and going astern fast, could be seen the sailor. He had caught the life buoy and was clinging to it. Nobody spoke. Nobody moved. The men aloft clung to the royal yards and watched with terror-stricken faces. And the *Mary Rogers* raced on, making her westing. A long, silent minute passed.

"Who was it?" Captain Cullen demanded.

"Mops, sir," eagerly answered the sailor at the wheel.

Mops topped a wave astern and disappeared temporarily in the trough. It was a large wave, but it was no graybeard. A small boat could live easily in such a sea, and in such a sea the *Mary Rogers* could easily come to. But she could not come to and make westing at the same time.

For the first time in all his years, George Dorety was seeing a real drama of life and death—a sordid little drama in which the scales balanced an un-known sailor named Mops against a few miles of longitude. At first he had watched the man astern, but now he watched big Dan Cullen, hairy and black, vested with power of life and death, smoking a cigar.

Captain Dan Cullen smoked another long, silent minute. Then he removed the cigar from his mouth. He glanced aloft at the spars of the *Mary Rogers*, and overside at the sea.

"Sheet home the royals!" he cried.

Fifteen minutes later they sat at table, in the cabin, with food served before them. On one side of George Dorety sat Dan Cullen, the tiger, on the other side, Joshua Higgins, the hyena. Nobody spoke. On deck the men were sheeting home the skysails. George Dorety could hear their cries, while a persistent vision haunted him of a man called Mops, alive and well, clinging to a life buoy miles astern in that lonely ocean. He glanced at Captain Cullen, and experienced a feeling of nausea, for the man was eating his food with relish, almost bolting it.

"Captain Cullen," Dorety said, "you are in command of this ship, and it is not proper for me to comment now upon what you do. But I wish to say one thing. There is a hereafter, and yours will be a hot one."

Captain Cullen did not even scowl. In his voice was regret as he said:—

"It was blowing a living gale. It was impossible to save the man."

"He fell from the royal-yard," Dorety cried hotly. "You were setting the royals at the time. Fifteen minutes afterward you were setting the skysails."

"It was a living gale, wasn't it, Mr. Higgins?" Captain Cullen said, turning to the mate.

"If you'd brought her to, it'd have taken the sticks out of her," was the mate's answer. "You did the proper thing, Captain Cullen The man hadn't a ghost of a show."

George Dorety made no answer, and to the meal's end no one spoke. After that, Dorety had his meals served in his stateroom. Captain Cullen scowled at him no longer, though no speech was exchanged between them, while the *Mary Rogers* sped north toward warmer latitudes. At the end of the week, Dan Cullen cornered Dorety on deck.

"What are you going to do when we get to 'Frisco?" he demanded bluntly.

"I am going to swear out a warrant for your arrest," Dorety answered quietly. "I am going to charge you with murder, and I am going to see you hanged for it."

"You're almighty sure of yourself," Captain Cullen sneered, turning on his heel.

A second week passed, and one morning found George Dorety standing in the coach-house companionway at the for'ard end of the long poop, taking his first gaze around the deck. The *Mary Rogers* was reaching full-and-by, in a stiff breeze. Every sail was set and drawing, including the staysails. Captain Cullen strolled for'ard along the poop. He strolled carelessly, glancing at the passenger out of the corner of his eye. Dorety was looking the other way, standing with head and shoulders outside the companionway, and only the back of his head was to be seen. Captain Cullen, with swift eye, embraced the mainstaysail-block and the head and estimated the distance. He glanced about him. Nobody was looking. Aft, Joshua Higgins, pacing up and down, had just turned his back and was going the other way. Captain Cullen bent over suddenly and cast the staysail-sheet off from its pin. The heavy block hurtled through the air, smashing Dorety's head like an egg-shell and hurtling on and back and forth as the staysail whipped and slatted in the wind. Joshua Higgins turned around to see what had carried away, and met the full blast of the vilest portion of Captain Cullen's profanity.

"I made the sheet fast myself," whimpered the mate in the first lull, "with an extra turn to make sure. I remember it distinctly."

"Made fast?" the Captain snarled back, for the benefit of the watch as it struggled to capture the flying sail before it tore to ribbons. "You couldn't make your grandmother fast, you useless hell's scullion. If you made that sheet fast with an extra turn, why in hell didn't it stay fast? That's what I want to know. Why in hell didn't it stay fast?"

The mate whined inarticulately.

"Oh, shut up!" was the final word of Captain Cullen.

Half an hour later he was as surprised as any when the body of George Dorety was found inside the companionway on the floor. In the afternoon, alone in his room, he doctored up the log.

"Ordinary seaman, Karl Brun," he wrote, *"lost overboard from foreroyal-yard in a gale of wind. Was running*

at the time, and for the safety of the ship did not dare come up to the wind. Nor could a boat have lived in the sea that was running."

On another page, he wrote:—

"Had often warned Mr. Dorety about the danger he ran because of his carelessness on deck. I told him, once, that some day he would get his head knocked off by a block. A carelessly fastened mainstaysail sheet was the cause of the accident, which was deeply to be regretted because Mr. Dorety was a favorite with all of us."

Captain Dan Cullen read over his literary effort with admiration, blotted the page, and closed the log. He lighted a cigar and stared before him. He felt the *Mary Rogers* lift, and heel, and surge along, and knew that she was making nine knots. A smile of satisfaction slowly dawned on his black and hairy face. Well, anyway, he had made his westing and fooled God.

SEMPER IDEM

Doctor Bicknell was in a remarkably gracious mood. Through a minor accident, a slight bit of carelessness, that was all, a man who might have pulled through had died the preceding night. Though it had been only a sailorman, one of the innumerable unwashed, the steward of the receiving hospital had been on the anxious seat all the morning. It was not that the man had died that gave him discomfort, he knew the Doctor too well for that, but his distress lay in the fact that the operation had been done so well. One of the most delicate in surgery, it had been as successful as it was clever and audacious. All had then depended upon the treatment, the nurses, the steward. And the man had died. Nothing much, a bit of carelessness, yet enough to bring the professional wrath of Doctor Bicknell about his ears and to perturb the working of the staff and nurses for twenty-four hours to come.

But, as already stated, the Doctor was in a

remarkably gracious mood. When informed by the steward, in fear and trembling, of the man's unexpected take-off, his lips did not so much as form one syllable of censure; nay, they were so pursed that snatches of rag-time floated softly from them, to be broken only by a pleasant query after the health of the other's eldest-born. The steward, deeming it impossible that he could have caught the gist of the case, repeated it.

"Yes, yes," Doctor Bicknell said impatiently; "I understand. But how about Semper Idem? Is he ready to leave?"

"Yes. They're helping him dress now," the steward answered, passing on to the round of his duties, content that peace still reigned within the iodine-saturated walls.

It was Semper Idem's recovery which had so fully compensated Doctor Bicknell for the loss of the sailorman. Lives were to him as nothing, the unpleasant but inevitable incidents of the profession, but cases, ah, cases were everything. People who knew him were prone to brand him a butcher, but his colleagues were at one in the belief that a bolder and yet a more capable man never stood over the table. He was not an imaginative man. He did not possess, and hence had no tolerance for, emotion. His nature was accurate, precise, scientific. Men were to him no more than pawns, without individuality or personal value. But as cases it was different. The more broken a man was, the more precarious his grip on life, the greater his significance in the eyes of Doctor Bicknell. He would as readily forsake a poet laureate suffering from a common accident for a nameless, mangled vagrant who defied every law of life by refusing to die, as would a child forsake a Punch and Judy for a circus.

So it had been in the case of Semper Idem. The mystery of the man had not appealed to him, nor had his silence and the veiled romance which the yellow reporters had so sensationally and so fruitlessly exploited in divers Sunday editions. But Semper Idem's throat had been cut. That was the point. That was where his interest had centred. Cut from ear to ear, and not one surgeon in a thousand to give a snap of the fingers for his chance of recovery. But, thanks to the swift municipal ambulance service and to Doctor Bicknell, he had been dragged back into the world he had sought to leave.

The Doctor's co-workers had shaken their heads when the case was brought in. Impossible, they said. Throat, windpipe, jugular, all but actually severed, and the loss of blood frightful. As it was such a foregone conclusion, Doctor Bicknell had employed methods and done things which made them, even in their professional capacities, to shudder. And lo! the man had recovered.

So, on this morning that Semper Idem was to leave the hospital, hale and hearty, Doctor Bicknell's geniality was in nowise disturbed by the steward's report, and he proceeded cheerfully to bring order out of the chaos of a child's body which had been ground and crunched beneath the wheels of an electric car.

As many will remember, the case of Semper Idem aroused a vast deal of unseemly yet highly natural curiosity. He had been found in a slum lodging, with throat cut as aforementioned, and blood dripping down upon the inmates of the room below and disturbing their festivities. He had evidently done the deed standing, with head bowed forward that he might gaze his last upon a photograph which stood on the table propped against a candlestick. It was this attitude which had made it possible for Doctor Bick-nell to save him. So terrific had been the sweep of the razor that had he had his head thrown back, as he should have done to have accomplished the act properly, with his neck stretched and the elastic vas-cular walls distended, he would have of a certainty well nigh decapitated himself.

At the hospital, during all the time he travelled the repugnant road back to life, not a word had left his lips. Nor could anything be learned of him by the sleuths detailed by the chief of police. Nobody knew him, nor had ever seen or heard of him before. He was strictly, uniquely, of the present. His clothes and surroundings were those of the lowest laborer, his hands the hands of a gentleman. But not a shred of writing was discovered, nothing, save in one par-ticular, which would serve to indicate his past or his position in life.

And that one particular was the photograph. If it were at all a likeness, the woman who gazed frankly out upon the onlooker from the card-mount must have been a striking creature indeed. It was an ama-teur production, for the detectives were baffled in that no professional photographer's signature or studio was appended. Across a corner of the mount, in delicate feminine tracery, was written: *"Semper idem; semper fidelis."* And she looked it. As many recollect, it was a face one could never forget. Clever halftones, remarkably like, were published in all the leading papers at the time; but such procedure gave rise to nothing but the uncontrollable public curiosity and interminable copy to the space-writers.

For want of a better name, the rescued suicide was known to the hospital attendants, and to the world, as Semper Idem. And Semper Idem he remained. Reporters, detectives, and nurses gave him up in despair. Not one word could he be persuaded to utter; yet the flitting conscious light of his eyes showed that his ears heard and his brain grasped every question put to him.

But this mystery and romance played no part in Doctor Bicknell's interest when he paused in the office to have a parting word with his patient. He, the Doctor, had performed a prodigy in the matter of this man, done what was virtually unprecedented in the annals of surgery. He did not care who or what the man was, and it was highly improbable that he should ever see him again; but, like the artist gazing upon a finished creation, he wished to look for the last time upon the work of his hand and brain.

Semper Idem still remained mute. He seemed anxious to be gone. Not a word could the Doctor extract from him, and little the Doctor cared. He examined the throat of the convalescent carefully, idling over the hideous scar with the lingering, half-caressing fondness of a parent. It was not a particularly pleasing sight. An angry line circled the throat, —for all the world as though the man had just escaped the hangman's noose, and,—disappearing below the ear on either side, had the appearance of completing the fiery periphery at the nape of the neck.

Maintaining his dogged silence, yielding to the other's examination in much the manner of a leashed lion, Semper Idem betrayed only his desire to drop from out of the public eye.

"Well, I'll not keep you," Doctor Bicknell finally said, laying a hand on the man's shoulder and stealing a last glance at his own handiwork. "But let me give you a bit of advice. Next time you try it on, hold your chin up, so. Don't snuggle it down and butcher yourself like a cow. Neatness and despatch, you know. Neatness and despatch."

Semper Idem's eyes flashed in token that he heard, and a moment later the hospital door swung to on his heel.

It was a busy day for Doctor Bicknell, and the afternoon was well along when he lighted a cigar preparatory to leaving the table upon which it seemed the sufferers almost clamored to be laid. But the last one, an old rag-picker with a broken shoulder-blade, had been disposed of, and the first fragrant smoke wreaths had begun to curl about his head, when the gong of a hurrying ambulance came through the open window from the street, followed by the inevitable entry of the stretcher with its ghastly freight.

"Lay it on the table," the Doctor directed, turning for a moment to place his cigar in safety. "What is it?"

"Suicide—throat cut," responded one of the stretcher bearers. "Down on Morgan Alley. Little hope, I think, sir. He's 'most gone."

"Eh? Well, I'll give him a look, anyway." He leaned over the man at the moment when the quick made its last faint flutter and succumbed.

"It's Semper Idem come back again," the steward said.

"Ay," replied Doctor Bicknell, "and gone again. No bungling this time. Properly done, upon my life, sir, properly done. Took my advice to the letter. I'm not required here. Take it along to the morgue."

Doctor Bicknell secured his cigar and relighted it. "That," he said between the puffs, looking at the steward, "that evens up for the one you lost last night. We're quits now."

A NOSE
FOR THE KING

In the morning calm of Korea, when its peace and tranquillity truly merited its ancient name, "Cho-sen," there lived a politician by name Yi Chin Ho. He was a man of parts, and—who shall say?—perhaps in no wise worse than politicians the world over. But, unlike his brethren in other lands, Yi Chin Ho was in jail. Not that he had inadvertently diverted to himself public moneys, but that he had inadvertently diverted too much. Excess is to be deplored in all things, even in grafting, and Yi Chin Ho's excess had brought him to most deplorable straits.

Ten thousand strings of cash he owed the government, and he lay in prison under sentence of death. There was one advantage to the situation—he had plenty of time in which to think. And he thought well. Then called he the jailer to him.

"Most worthy man, you see before you one most wretched" he began. "Yet all will be well with me if you will but let me go free for one short hour this night. And all will be well with you, for I shall see to your advancement through the years, and you shall come at length to the directorship of all the prisons of Cho-sen."

"How, now?" demanded the jailer. "What foolishness is this? One short hour, and you but waiting for your head to be chopped off! And I, with an aged and much-to-be-respected mother, not to say anything of a wife and several children of tender years! Out upon you for the scoundrel that you are!"

"From the Sacred City to the ends of all the Eight Coasts there is no place for me to hide," Yi Chin Ho made reply. "I am a man of wisdom, but of what worth my wisdom here in prison? Were I free, well I know I could seek out and obtain the money wherewith to repay the government. I know of a nose that will save me from all my difficulties."

"A nose!" cried the jailer.

"A nose," said Yi Chin Ho. "A remarkable nose, if I may say so, a most remarkable nose."

The jailer threw up his hands despairingly. "Ah,

what a wag you are, what a wag," he laughed. "To think that that very admirable wit of yours must go the way of the chopping-block!"

And so saying, he turned and went away. But in the end, being a man soft of head and heart, when the night was well along he permitted Yi Chin Ho to go.

Straight he went to the Governor, catching him alone and arousing him from his sleep.

"Yi Chin Ho, or I'm no Governor!" cried the Governor. "What do you here who should be in prison waiting on the chopping-block?"

"I pray your excellency to listen to me," said Yi Chin Ho, squatting on his hams by the bedside and lighting his pipe from the fire-box. "A dead man is without value. It is true, I am as a dead man, without value to the government, to your excellency, or to myself. But if, so to say, your excellency were to give me my freedom—"

"Impossible!" cried the Governor. "Besides, you are condemned to death."

"Your excellency well knows that if I can repay the ten thousand strings of cash, the government will pardon me," Yi Chin Ho went on. "So, as I say, if your excellency were to give me my freedom for a few days, being a man of understanding, I should then repay the government and be in position to be of service to your excellency. I should be in position to be of very great service to your excellency."

"Have you a plan whereby you hope to obtain this money?" asked the Governor.

"I have," said Yi Chin Ho.

"Then come with it to me to-morrow night; I would now sleep," said the Governor, taking up his snore where it had been interrupted.

On the following night, having again obtained leave of absence from the jailer, Yi Chin Ho presented himself at the Governor's bedside.

"Is it you, Yi Chin Ho?" asked the Governor. "And have you the plan?"

"It is I, your excellency," answered Yi Chin Ho, "and the plan is here."

"Speak," commanded the Governor.

"The plan is here," repeated Yi Chin Ho, "here in my hand."

The Governor sat up and opened his eyes. Yi Chin Ho proffered in his hand a sheet of paper. The Governor held it to the light.

"Nothing but a nose," said he.

"A bit pinched, so, and so, your excellency," said Yi Chin Ho.

"Yes, a bit pinched here and there, as you say," said the Governor.

"Withal it is an exceeding corpulent nose, thus, and so, all in one place, at the end," proceeded Yi Chin Ho. "Your excellency would seek far and wide and many a day for that nose and find it not."

"An unusual nose," admitted the Governor.

"There is a wart upon it," said Yi Chin Ho.

"A most unusual nose," said the Governor. "Never have I seen the like. But what do you with this nose, Yi Chin Ho?"

"I seek it whereby to repay the money to the government," said Yi Chin Ho. "I seek it to be of service to your excellency, and I seek it to save my own worthless head. Further, I seek your excellency's seal upon this picture of the nose."

And the Governor laughed and affixed the seal of state, and Yi Chin Ho departed. For a month and a day he travelled the King's Road which leads to the shore of the Eastern Sea; and there, one night, at the gate of the largest mansion of a wealthy city he knocked loudly for admittance.

"None other than the master of the house will I see," said he fiercely to the frightened servants. "I travel upon the King's business."

Straightway was he led to an inner room, where the master of the house was roused from his sleep and brought blinking before him.

"You are Pak Chung Chang, head man of this city," said Yi Chin Ho in tones that were all-accusing. "I am upon the King's business."

Pak Chung Chang trembled. Well he knew the King's business was ever a terrible business. His knees smote together, and he near fell to the floor.

"The hour is late," he quavered. "Were it not well to—"

"The King's business never waits!" thundered Yi Chin Ho. "Come apart with me, and swiftly. I have an affair of moment to discuss with you.

"It is the King's affair," he added with even greater fierceness; so that Pak Chung Chang's silver pipe dropped from his nerveless fingers and clattered on the floor.

"Know then," said Yi Chin Ho, when they had gone apart, "that the King is troubled with an affliction, a very terrible affliction. In that he failed to cure, the Court physician has had nothing else than his head chopped off. From all the Eight Provinces have the physicians come to wait upon the King. Wise consultation have they held, and they have decided that for a remedy for the King's affliction nothing else is required than a nose, a certain kind of nose, a very peculiar certain kind of nose.

"Then by none other was I summoned than his excellency the prime minister himself. He put a paper into my hand. Upon this paper was the very peculiar kind of nose drawn by the physicians of the Eight Provinces, with the seal of state upon it.

"'Go,' said his excellency the prime minister. 'Seek out this nose, for the King's affliction is sore. And wheresoever you find this nose upon the face of a man, strike it off forthright and bring it in all haste to the Court, for the King must be cured. Go, and come not back until your search is rewarded.'

"And so I departed upon my quest," said Yi Chin Ho. "I have sought out the remotest corners of the kingdom; I have travelled the Eight Highways, searched the Eight Provinces, and sailed the seas of the Eight Coasts. And here I am."

With a great flourish he drew a paper from his

girdle, unrolled it with many snappings and crack-lings, and thrust it before the face of Pak Chung Chang. Upon the paper was the picture of the nose.

Pak Chung Chang stared upon it with bulging eyes.

"Never have I beheld such a nose," he began.

"There is a wart upon it," said Yi Chin Ho.

"Never have I beheld—" Pak Chung Chang began again.

"Bring your father before me," Yi Chin Ho inter-rupted sternly.

"My ancient and very-much-to-be-respected ancestor sleeps," said Pak Chung Chang.

"Why dissemble?" demanded Yi Chin Ho. "You know it is your father's nose. Bring him before me that I may strike it off and be gone. Hurry, lest I make bad report of you."

"Mercy!" cried Pak Chung Chang, falling on his knees. "It is impossible! It is impossible! You cannot strike off my father's nose. He cannot go down without his nose to the grave. He will become a laughter and a byword, and all my days and nights will be filled with woe. O reflect! Report that you have seen no such nose in your travels. You, too, have a father."

Pak Chung Chang clasped Yi Chin Ho's knees and fell to weeping on his sandals.

"My heart softens strangely at your tears," said Yi Chin Ho. "I, too, know filial piety and regard. But—" He hesitated, then added, as though thinking aloud, "It is as much as my head is worth."

"How much is your head worth?" asked Pak Chung Chang in a thin, small voice.

"A not remarkable head," said Yi Chin Ho. "An absurdly unremarkable head; but, such is my great foolishness, I value it at nothing less than one hundred thousand strings of cash."

"So be it," said Pak Chung Chang, rising to his feet.

"I shall need horses to carry the treasure," said Yi Chin Ho, "and men to guard it well as I journey through the mountains. There are robbers abroad in the land."

"There are robbers abroad in the land," said Pak Chung Chang, sadly. "But it shall be as you wish, so long as my ancient and very-much-to-be-respected ancestor's nose abide in its appointed place."

"Say nothing to any man of this occurrence," said Yi Chin Ho, "else will other and more loyal servants than I be sent to strike off your father's nose."

And so Yi Chin Ho departed on his way through the mountains, blithe of heart and gay of song as he listened to the jingling bells of his treasure-laden ponies.

There is little more to tell. Yi Chin Ho prospered through the years. By his efforts the jailer attained at length to the directorship of all the prisons of Chosen; the Governor ultimately betook himself to the Sacred City to be prime minister to the King, while Yi Chin Ho became the King's boon companion and sat at table with him to the end of a round, fat life. But Pak Chung Chang fell into a melancholy, and ever after he shook his head sadly, with tears in his eyes, whenever he regarded the expensive nose of his ancient and very-much-to-be-respected ancestor.

THE "FRANCIS SPAIGHT"

(A TRUE TALE RETOLD)

The *Francis Spaight* was running before it solely under a mizzentopsail, when the thing happened. It was not due to carelessness so much as to the lack of discipline of the crew and to the fact that they were indifferent seamen at best. The man at the wheel in particular, a Limerick man, had had no experience with salt water beyond that of rafting timber on the Shannon between the Quebec vessels and the shore. He was afraid of the huge seas that rose out of the murk astern and bore down upon him, and he was more given to cowering away from their threatened impact than he was to meeting their blows with the wheel and checking the ship's rush to broach to.

It was three in the morning when his un-seamanlike conduct precipitated the catastrophe. At sight of a sea far larger than its fellows, he crouched down, releasing his hands from the spokes. The *Francis Spaight* sheered as her stern lifted on the sea, receiving the full fling of the cap on her quarter. The next instant she was in the trough, her lee-rail buried till the ocean was level with her hatch-combings, sea after sea breaking over her weather rail and sweeping what remained exposed of the deck with icy deluges.

The men were out of hand, helpless and hopeless, stupid in their bewilderment and fear, and resolute only in that they would not obey orders. Some wailed, others clung silently in the weather shrouds, and still others muttered prayers or shrieked vile imprecations; and neither captain nor mate could get them to bear a hand at the pumps or at setting patches of sails to bring the vessel up to the wind and sea. Inside the hour the ship was over on her beam ends, the lubberly cowards climbing up her side and hanging on in the rigging. When she went over, the mate was caught and drowned in the after-cabin, as were two sailors who had sought refuge in the forecastle.

The mate had been the ablest man on board, and the captain was now scarcely less helpless than his men. Beyond cursing them for their worthlessness, he did nothing; and it remained for a man named Mahoney, a Belfast man, and a boy, O'Brien, of Limerick, to cut away the fore and main masts. This they did at great risk on the perpendicular wall of the wreck, sending the mizzentopmast overside along in the general crash. The *Francis Spaight* righted, and it was well that she was lumber laden, else she would have sunk, for she was already water-logged. The mainmast, still fast by the shrouds, beat like a thunderous sledge-hammer against the ship's side, every stroke bringing groans from the men.

Day dawned on the savage ocean, and in the cold gray light all that could be seen of the *Francis Spaight* emerging from the sea were the poop, the shattered mizzenmast, and a ragged line of bulwarks. It was midwinter in the North Atlantic, and the wretched men were half-dead from cold. But there was no place where they could find rest. Every sea breached clean over the wreck, washing away the salt incrustations from their bodies and depositing fresh incrustations. The cabin under the poop was awash to the knees, but here at least was shelter from the chill wind, and here the survivors congregated, standing upright, holding on by the cabin furnishings, and leaning against one another for support.

In vain Mahoney strove to get the men to take turns in watching aloft from the mizzenmast for any chance vessel. The icy gale was too much for them, and they preferred the shelter of the cabin. O'Brien, the boy, who was only fifteen, took turns with Mahoney on the freezing perch. It was the boy, at three in the afternoon, who called down that he had sighted a sail. This did bring them from the cabin, and they crowded the poop rail and weather mizzen shrouds as they watched the strange ship. But its course did not lie near, and when it disappeared below the skyline, they returned shivering to the cabin, not one offering to relieve the watch at the masthead.

By the end of the second day, Mahoney and O'Brien gave up their attempt, and thereafter the vessel drifted in the gale uncared for and without a lookout. There were thirteen alive, and for seventy-two hours they stood knee-deep in the sloshing water on the cabin floor, half-frozen, without food, and with but three bottles of wine shared among them. All food and fresh water were below, and there was no getting at such supplies in the water-logged condition of the wreck. As the days went by, no food whatever passed their lips. Fresh water, in small quantities, they were able to obtain by holding a cover of a tureen under the saddle of the mizzen-mast. But the rain fell infrequently, and they were hard put. When it rained, they also soaked their handkerchiefs, squeezing them out into their mouths or into their shoes. As the wind and sea went down, they were even able to mop the exposed portions of the deck that were free from brine and so add to their water supply. But food they had none, and no way of getting it, though sea-birds flew repeatedly overhead.

In the calm weather that followed the gale, after having remained on their feet for ninety-six hours, they were able to find dry planks in the cabin on which to lie. But the long hours of standing in the salt water had caused sores to form on their legs. These sores were extremely painful. The slightest contact or scrape caused severe anguish, and in their weak condition and crowded situation they were continually hurting one another in this manner. Not a man could move about without being followed by volleys of abuse, curses, and groans. So great was their misery that the strong oppressed the weak, shoving them aside from the dry planks to shift for themselves in the cold and wet. The boy, O'Brien, was specially maltreated. Though there were three other boys, it was O'Brien who came in for most of the abuse. There was no explaining it, except on the ground that his was a stronger and more dominant spirit than those of the other boys, and that he stood up more for his rights, resenting the petty injustices that were meted out to all the boys by the men. Whenever O'Brien came near the men in search of a dry place to sleep, or merely moved about, he was kicked and cuffed away. In return, he cursed them for their selfish brutishness, and blows and kicks and curses were rained upon him. Miserable as were all of them, he was thus made far more miserable; and it was only the flame of life, unusually strong in him, that enabled him to endure.

As the days went by and they grew weaker, their peevishness and ill-temper increased, which, in turn, increased the ill-treatment and sufferings of O'Brien. By the sixteenth day all hands were far gone with hunger, and they stood together in small groups, talking in undertones and occasionally glancing at O'Brien. It was at high noon that the conference came to a head. The captain was the spokesman. All were collected on the poop.

"Men," the captain began, "we have been a long time without food—two weeks and two days it is, though it seems more like two years and two months. We can't hang out much longer. It is beyond human nature to go on hanging out with nothing in our stomachs. There is a serious question to consider: whether it is better for all to die, or for one to die. We are standing with our feet in our graves. If one of us dies, the rest may live until a ship is sighted. What say you?"

Michael Behane, the man who had been at the wheel when the *Francis Spaight* broached to, called out that it was well. The others joined in the cry.

"Let it be one of the b'ys !" cried Sullivan, a Tarbert man, glancing at the same time significantly at O'Brien.

"It is my opinion," the captain went on, "that it will be a good deed for one of us to die for the rest."

"A good deed! A good deed!" the men interjected.

"And it is my opinion that 'tis best for one of the boys to die. They have no families to support, nor would they be considered so great a loss to their friends as those who have wives and children."

"'Tis right." "Very right." "Very fit it should be done," the men muttered one to another.

But the four boys cried out against the injustice of it.

"Our lives is just as dear to us as the rest iv yez," O'Brien protested. "An' our famblies, too. As for wives an' childer, who is there savin' meself to care for me old mother that's a widow, as you know well, Michael Behane, that comes from Limerick? 'Tis not fair. Let the lots be drawn between all of us, men and b'ys."

Mahoney was the only man who spoke in favor of the boys, declaring that it was the fair thing for all to share alike. Sullivan and the captain insisted on the drawing of lots being confined to the boys. There were high words, in the midst of which Sullivan turned upon O'Brien, snarling:—

"'Twould be a good deed to put you out of the way. You deserve it. 'Twould be the right way to serve you, an' serve you we will."

He started toward O'Brien, with intent to lay hands on him and proceed at once with the killing, while several others likewise shuffled toward him and reached for him. He stumbled backwards to escape them, at the same time crying that he would submit to the drawing of the lots among the boys.

The captain prepared four sticks of different lengths and handed them to Sullivan.

"You're thinkin' the drawin'll not be fair," the latter sneered to O'Brien. "So it's yer-self'll do the drawin'."

To this O'Brien agreed. A handkerchief was tied over his eyes, blindfolding him, and he knelt down on the deck with his back to Sullivan.

"Whoever you name for the shortest stick'll die," the captain said.

Sullivan held up one of the sticks. The rest were concealed in his hand so that no one could see whether it was the short stick or not.

"An' whose stick will it be?" Sullivan demanded.

"For little Johnny Sheehan," O'Brien answered.

Sullivan laid the stick aside. Those who looked could not tell if it were the fatal one. Sullivan held up another stick.

"Whose will it be?"

"For George Burns," was the reply.

The stick was laid with the first one, and a third held up.

"An' whose is this wan?"

"For myself," said O'Brien.

With a quick movement, Sullivan threw the four sticks together. No one had seen.

"'Tis for yourself ye've drawn it," Sullivan announced.

"A good deed," several of the men muttered.

O'Brien was very quiet. He arose to his feet, took the bandage off, and looked around.

"Where is ut?" he demanded. "The short stick? The wan for me?"

The captain pointed to the four sticks lying on the deck.

"How do you know the stick was mine?" O'Brien questioned. "Did you see ut, Johnny Sheehan?"

Johnny Sheehan, who was the youngest of the boys, did not answer.

"Did you see ut?" O'Brien next asked Mahoney.

"No, I didn't see ut."

The men were muttering and growling.

"'Twas a fair drawin'," Sullivan said. "Ye had yer chanct an' ye lost, that's all iv ut."

"A fair drawin'," the captain added. "Didn't I behold it myself? The stick was yours, O'Brien, an' ye may as well get ready. Where's the cook? Gorman, come here. Fetch the tureen cover, some of ye. Gorman, do your duty like a man."

"But how'll I do it?" the cook demanded. He was a weak-eyed, weak-chinned, indecisive man.

"'Tis a damned murder!" O'Brien cried out.

"I'll have none of ut," Mahoney announced. "Not a bite shall pass me lips."

"Then 'tis yer share for better men than yerself," Sullivan sneered. "Go on with yer duty, cook."

"'Tis not me duty, the killin' of b'ys," Gorman protested irresolutely.

"If yez don't make mate for us, we'll be makin' mate of yerself," Behane threatened. "Somebody must die, an' as well you as another."

Johnny Sheehan began to cry. O'Brien listened anxiously. His face was pale. His lips trembled, and at times his whole body shook.

"I signed on as cook," Gorman enounced. "An' cook I wud if galley there was. But I'll not lay me hand to murder. 'Tis not in the articles. I'm the cook—"

"An' cook ye'll be for wan minute more only," Sullivan said grimly, at the same moment gripping the cook's head from behind and bending it back till the windpipe and jugular were stretched taut. "Where's yer knife, Mike? Pass it along."

At the touch of the steel, Gorman whimpered.

"I'll do ut, if yez'll hold the b'y."

The pitiable condition of the cook seemed in some fashion to nerve up O'Brien.

"It's all right, Gorman," he said. "Go on with ut. 'Tis meself knows yer not wantin' to do ut. It's all right, sir"—this to the captain, who had laid a hand heavily on his arm. "Ye won't have to hold me, sir. I'll stand still."

"Stop yer blitherin', an' go an' get the tureen cover," Behane commanded Johnny Sheehan, at the same time dealing him a heavy cuff alongside the head.

The boy, who was scarcely more than a child, fetched the cover. He crawled and tottered along the deck, so weak was he from hunger. The tears still ran down his cheeks. Behane took the cover from him, at the same time administering another cuff.

O'Brien took off his coat and bared his right arm. His under lip still trembled, but he held a tight grip on himself. The captain's penknife was opened and passed to Gorman.

"Mahoney, tell me mother what happened to me, if ever ye get back," O'Brien requested.

Mahoney nodded.

"'Tis black murder, black an' damned," he said. "The b'y's flesh'll do none iv yez anny good. Mark me words. Ye'll not profit by it, none iv yez."

"Get ready," the captain ordered. "You, Sullivan, hold the cover—that's it—close up. Spill nothing. It's precious stuff."

Gorman made an effort. The knife was dull. He was weak. Besides, his hand was shaking so violently that he nearly dropped the knife. The three boys were crouched apart, in a huddle, crying and sobbing. With the exception of Mahoney, the men were gathered about the victim, craning their necks to see.

"Be a man, Gorman," the captain cautioned.

The wretched cook was seized with a spasm of resolution, sawing back and forth with the blade on O'Brien's wrist. The veins were severed. Sullivan held the tureen cover close underneath. The cut veins gaped wide, but no ruddy flood gushed forth. There was no blood at all. The veins were dry and empty. No one spoke. The grim and silent figures swayed in unison with each heave of the ship. Every eye was turned fixedly upon that inconceivable and monstrous thing, the dry veins of a creature that was alive.

"'Tis a warnin'," Mahoney cried. "Lave the b'y alone. Mark me words. His death'll do none iv yez anny good."

"Try at the elbow—the left elbow, 'tis nearer the heart," the captain said finally, in a dim and husky voice that was unlike his own.

"Give me the knife," O'Brien said roughly, taking it out of the cook's hand. "I can't be lookin' at ye puttin' me to hurt."

Quite coolly he cut the vein at the left elbow, but, like the cook, he failed to bring blood.

"This is all iv no use," Sullivan said. "'Tis better to put him out iv his misery by bleedin' him at the throat."

The strain had been too much for the lad.

"Don't be doin' ut," he cried. "There'll be no blood in me throat. Give me a little time. 'Tis cold an' weak I am. Be lettin' me lay down an' slape a bit. Then I'll be warm an' the blood'll flow."

"'Tis no use," Sullivan objected. "As if ye cud be slapin' at a time like this. Ye'll not slape, and ye'll not warm up. Look at ye now. You've an ague."

"I was sick at Limerick wan night," O'Brien hurried on, "an' the dochtor cudn't bleed me. But after slapin' a few hours an' gettin' warm in bed the blood came freely. It's God's truth I'm tellin' yez. Don't be murderin' me!"

"His veins are open now," the captain said. "'Tis no use leavin' him in his pain. Do it now an' be done with it."

They started to reach for O'Brien, but he backed away.

"I'll be the death iv yez!" he screamed. "Take yer hands off iv me, Sullivan! I'll come back! I'll haunt yez! Wakin' or slapin', I'll haunt yez till you die!"

"'Tis disgraceful!" yelled Behane. "If the short stick'd ben mine, I'd a-let me mates cut the head off iv me an' died happy."

Sullivan leaped in and caught the unhappy lad by the hair. The rest of the men followed. O'Brien kicked and struggled, snarling and snapping at the hands that clutched him from every side. Little Johnny Sheehan broke out into wild screaming, but the men took no notice of him. O'Brien was bent backward to the deck, the tureen cover under his neck. Gorman was shoved forward. Some one had thrust a large sheath-knife into his hand.

"Do yer duty! Do yer duty!" the men cried.

The cook bent over, but he caught the boy's eye and faltered.

"If ye don't, I'll kill ye with me own hands," Behane shouted.

From every side a torrent of abuse and threats poured in upon the cook. Still he hung back.

"Maybe there'll be more blood in his veins than O'Brien's," Sullivan suggested significantly.

Behane caught Gorman by the hair and twisted his head back, while Sullivan attempted to take possession of the sheath-knife. But Gorman clung to it desperately.

"Lave go, an' I'll do ut!" he screamed frantically. "Don't be cuttin' me throat! I'll do the deed! I'll do the deed!"

"See that you do it, then," the captain threatened him.

Gorman allowed himself to be shoved forward. He looked at the boy, closed his eyes, and muttered a prayer. Then, without opening his eyes, he did the deed that had been appointed him. O'Brien emitted a shriek that sank swiftly to a gurgling sob. The men held him till his struggles ceased, when he was laid upon the deck. They were eager and impatient, and with oaths and threats they urged Gorman to hurry with the preparation of the meal.

"Lave ut, you bloody butchers," Mahoney said quietly. "Lave ut, I tell yez. Ye'll not be needin' anny iv ut now. 'Tis as I said; ye'll not be profitin' by the lad's blood. Empty ut overside, Behane. Empty ut overside."

Behane, still holding the tureen cover in both his hands, glanced to windward. He walked to the rail and threw the cover and contents into the sea. A full-rigged ship was bearing down upon them a short mile away. So occupied had they been with the deed just committed, that none had had eyes for a lookout. All hands watched her coming on—the brightly coppered forefoot parting the water like a golden knife, the headsails flapping lazily and emptily at each downward surge, and the towering canvas tiers dipping and courtesying with each stately swing of the sea. No man spoke.

As she hove to, a cable length away, the captain of the *Francis Spaight* bestirred himself and ordered a tarpaulin to be thrown over O'Brien's corpse. A boat was lowered from the stranger's side and began to pull toward them. John Gorman laughed. He laughed softly at first, but he accompanied each stroke of the oars with spasmodically increasing glee. It was this maniacal laughter that greeted the rescue boat as it hauled alongside and the first officer clambered on board.

A CURIOUS FRAGMENT

[*The capitalist, or industrial oligarch, Roger Vanderwater,*
mentioned in the narrative, has been identified as the ninth
in the line of the Vanderwaters that controlled for hundreds
of years the cotton factories of the South. This Roger Van-
derwater flourished in the last decades of the twenty-sixth
century after Christ, which was the fifth century of the ter-
rible industrial oligarchy that was reared upon the ruins of
the early Republic.

From internal evidences we are convinced that the nar-
rative which follows was not reduced to writing till the
twenty-ninth century. Not only was it unlawful to write or
print such matter during that period, but the working-class
was so illiterate that only in rare instances were its mem-
bers able to read and write. This was the dark reign of the
overman, in whose speech the great mass of the people were
characterized as the "herd animals." All literacy was
frowned upon and stamped out. From the statute-books of
the times may be instanced that black law that made it a

capital offence for any man, no matter of what class, to teach even the alphabet to a member of the working-class. Such stringent limitation of education to the ruling class was necessary if that class was to continue to rule.

*One result of the foregoing was the development of the professional story-tellers. These story-tellers were paid by the oligarchy, and the tales they told were legendary, mythical, romantic, and harmless. But the spirit of freedom never quite died out, and agitators, under the guise of story-tellers, preached revolt to the slave class. That the following tale was banned by the oligarchs we have proof from the records of the criminal police court of Ashbury, wherein, on January 27, 2734, one John Tourney, found guilty of telling the tale in a boozing-ken of laborers, was sentenced to five years' penal servitude in the borax mines of the Arizona Desert.—*EDITOR'S NOTE.]

A CURIOUS FRAGMENT

Listen, my brothers, and I will tell you a tale of an arm. It was the arm of Tom Dixon, and Tom Dixon was a weaver of the first class in a factory of that hell-hound and master, Roger Vanderwater.

This factory was called "Hell's Bottom"...by the slaves who toiled in it, and I guess they ought to know; and it was situated in Kingsbury, at the other end of the town from Vanderwater's summer palace. You do not know where Kingsbury is? There are many things, my brothers, that you do not know, and it is sad. It is because you do not know that you are slaves. When I have told you this tale, I should like to form a class among you for the learning of written and printed speech. Our masters read and write and possess many books, and it is because of that that they are our masters, and live in palaces, and do not work. When the toilers learn to read and write,—all of them—they will grow strong; then they will use their strength to break their bonds, and there will be no more masters and no more slaves.

Kingsbury, my brothers, is in the old State of Alabama. For three hundred years the Vanderwaters have owned Kingsbury and its slave pens and factories, and slave pens and factories in many other places and States. You have heard of the Vanderwaters,—who has not?—but let me tell you things you do not know about them. The first Vanderwater was a slave, even as you and I. Have you got that? He was a slave, and that was over three hundred years ago. His father was a machinist in the slave pen of Alexander Burrell, and his mother was a washer-woman in the same slave pen. There is no doubt about this. I am telling you truth. It is history. It is printed, every word of it, in the history books of our masters, which you cannot read because your masters will not permit you to learn to read. You can understand why they will not permit you to learn to read, when there are such things in the books. They know, and they are very wise. If you did read such things, you might be wanting in respect to your masters, which would be a dangerous thing...to your masters. But I know, for I can read, and I am telling you what I have read with my own eyes in the history books of our masters.

The first Vanderwater's name was not Vanderwater; it was Vange—Bill Vange, the son of Yergis Vange, the machinist, and Laura Carnly, the washerwoman. Young Bill Vange was strong. He might have remained with the slaves and led them to freedom; instead, however, he served the masters and was well rewarded. He began his service, when yet a small child, as a spy in his home slave pen. He is known to have informed on his own father for seditious utterance. This is fact. I have read it with my own eyes in the records. He was too good a slave for the slave pen. Alexander Burrell took him out, while yet a child, and he was taught to read and write. He was taught many things, and he was entered in the secret service of the government. Of course, he no longer wore the slave dress, except for disguise at such times when he sought to penetrate the secrets and plots of the slaves. It was he, when but eighteen years of age, who brought that great hero and comrade, Ralph Jacobus, to trial and execution in the electric chair. Of course, you have all heard the sacred name of Ralph Jacobus, but it is news to you that he was brought to his death by the first Vanderwater, whose name was Vange. I know. I have read it in the books. There are many interesting things like that in the books.

And after Ralph Jacobus died his shameful death, Bill Vange's name began the many changes it was to undergo. He was known as "Sly Vange" far and wide. He rose high in the secret service, and he was rewarded in grand ways, but still he was not a member of the master class. The men were willing

that he should become so; it was the women of the
master class who refused to have Sly Vange one of
them. Sly Vange gave good service to the masters.
He had been a slave himself, and he knew the ways
of the slaves. There was no fooling him. In those
days the slaves were braver than now, and they were
always trying for their freedom. And Sly Vange was
everywhere, in all their schemes and plans, bringing
their schemes and plans to naught and their leaders
to the electric chair. It was in 2255 that his name was
next changed for him. It was in that year that the
Great Mutiny took place. In that region west of the
Rocky Mountains, seventeen millions of slaves
strove bravely to overthrow their masters. Who
knows, if Sly Vange had not lived, but that they
would have succeeded? But Sly Vange was very
much alive. The masters gave him supreme command of the situation. In eight months of fighting,
one million and three hundred and fifty thousand
slaves were killed. Vange, Bill Vange, Sly Vange,
killed them, and he broke the Great Mutiny. And he
was greatly rewarded, and so red were his hands
with the blood of the slaves that thereafter he was
called "Bloody Vange." You see, my brothers, what

interesting things are to be found in the books when one can read them. And, take my word for it, there are many other things, even more interesting, in the books. And if you will but study with me, in a year's time you can read those books for yourselves—ay, in six months some of you will be able to read those books for yourselves.

Bloody Vange lived to a ripe old age, and always, to the last, was he received in the councils of the masters; but never was he made a master himself. He had first opened his eyes, you see, in a slave pen. But oh, he was well rewarded! He had a dozen palaces in which to live. He, who was no master, owned thousands of slaves. He had a great pleasure yacht upon the sea that was a floating palace, and he owned a whole island in the sea where toiled ten thousand slaves on his coffee plantations. But in his old age he was lonely, for he lived apart, hated by his brothers, the slaves, and looked down upon by those he had served and who refused to be his brothers. The masters looked down upon him because he had been born a slave. Enormously wealthy he died; but he died horribly, tormented by his conscience, regretting all he had done and the red stain on his name.

But with his children it was different. They had not been born in the slave pen, and by the special ruling of the Chief Oligarch of that time, John Morrison, they were elevated to the master class. And it was then that the name of Vange disappears from the page of history. It becomes Vanderwater, and Jason Vange, the son of Bloody Vange, becomes Jason Vanderwater, the founder of the Vanderwater line. But that was three hundred years ago, and the Vanderwaters of to-day forget their beginnings and imagine that somehow the clay of their bodies is different stuff from the clay in your body and mine and in the bodies of all slaves. And I ask you, Why should a slave become the master of another slave? And why should the son of a slave become the master of many slaves? I leave these questions for you to answer for yourselves, but do not forget that in the beginning the Vanderwaters were slaves.

And now, my brothers, I come back to the beginning of my tale to tell you of Tom Dixon's arm. Roger Vanderwater's factory in Kingsbury was rightly named "Hell's Bottom," but the men who toiled in it were men, as you shall see. Women toiled there, too, and children, little children. All that toiled there had the regular slave rights under the law, but only under the law, for they were deprived of many of their rights by the two overseers of Hell's Bottom, Joseph Clancy and Adolph Munster.

It is a long story, but I shall not tell all of it to you. I shall tell only about the arm. It happened that, according to the law, a portion of the starvation wage of the slaves was held back each month and put into a fund. This fund was for the purpose of helping such unfortunate fellow-workmen as happened to be injured by accidents or to be overtaken by sickness. As you know with yourselves, these funds are controlled by the overseers. It is the law, and so it was that the fund at Hell's Bottom was controlled by the two overseers of accursed memory.

Now, Clancy and Munster took this fund for their own use. When accidents happened to the workmen, their fellows, as was the custom, made grants from the fund; but the overseers refused to pay over the grants. What could the slaves do? They had their rights under the law, but they had no access to the law. Those that complained to the overseers were punished. You know yourselves what form such punishment takes—the fines for faulty work that is not faulty; the overcharging of accounts in the Company's store; the vile treatment of one's women and children; and the allotment to bad machines whereon, work as one will, he starves.

Once, the slaves of Hell's Bottom protested to Vanderwater. It was the time of the year when he spent several months in Kingsbury. One of the slaves could write; it chanced that his mother could write, and she had secretly taught him as her mother had secretly taught her. So this slave wrote a round robin, wherein was contained their grievances, and all the slaves signed by mark. And, with proper stamps upon the envelope, the round robin was mailed to Roger Vanderwater. And Roger Vanderwater did nothing, save to turn the round robin over to the two overseers. Clancy and Munster were angered. They turned the guards loose at night on the slave pen. The guards were armed with pick handles. It is said that next day only half of the slaves were able to work in Hell's Bottom. They were well beaten. The slave who could write was so badly beaten that he lived only three months. But before he died, he wrote once more, to what purpose you shall hear.

A Curious Fragment

Four or five weeks afterward, Tom Dixon, a slave, had his arm torn off by a belt in Hell's Bottom. His fellow-workmen, as usual, made a grant to him from the fund, and Clancy and Munster, as usual, refused to pay it over from the fund. The slave who could write, and who even then was dying, wrote anew a recital of their grievances. And this document was thrust into the hand of the arm that had been torn from Tom Dixon's body.

Now it chanced that Roger Vanderwater was lying ill in his palace at the other end of Kingsbury—not the dire illness that strikes down you and me, brothers; just a bit of biliousness, mayhap, or no more than a bad headache because he had eaten too heartily or drunk too deeply. But it was enough for him, being tender and soft from careful rearing. Such men, packed in cotton wool all their lives, are exceeding tender and soft. Believe me, brothers, Roger Vanderwater felt as badly with his aching head, or *thought* he felt as badly, as Tom Dixon really felt with his arm torn out by the roots.

It happened that Roger Vanderwater was fond of scientific farming, and that on his farm, three miles outside of Kingsbury, he had managed to grow a new kind of strawberry. He was very proud of that new strawberry of his, and he would have been out to see and pick the first ripe ones, had it not been for his illness. Because of his illness he had ordered the old farm slave to bring in personally the first box of the berries. All this was learned from the gossip of a palace scullion, who slept each night in the slave pen. The overseer of the plantation should have brought in the berries, but he was on his back with a broken leg from trying to break a colt. The scullion brought the word in the night, and it was known that next day the berries would come in. And the men in the slave pen of Hell's Bottom, being men and not cowards, held a council.

The slave who could write, and who was sick and dying from the pick-handle beating, said he would carry Tom Dixon's arm; also, he said he must die anyway, and that it mattered nothing if he died a little sooner. So five slaves stole from the slave pen that night after the guards had made their last rounds. One of the slaves was the man who could write. They lay in the brush by the roadside until late in the morning, when the old farm slave came driving to town with the precious fruit for the master. What of the farm slave being old and rheumatic, and of the slave who could write being stiff and injured from his beating, they moved their bodies about when they walked, very much in the same fashion. The slave who could write put on the other's clothes, pulled the broad-brimmed hat over his eyes, climbed upon the seat of the wagon, and drove on to town. The old farm slave was kept tied all day in the bushes until evening, when the others loosed him and went back to the slave pen to take their punishment for having broken bounds.

In the meantime, Roger Vanderwater lay waiting for the berries in his wonderful bedroom—such wonders and such comforts were there that they would have blinded the eyes of you and me who have never seen such things. The slave who could write said afterward that it was like a glimpse of Paradise. And why not? The labor and the lives of ten thousand slaves had gone to the making of that bed-chamber, while they themselves slept in vile lairs like wild beasts. The slave who could write brought in the berries on a silver tray or platter—you see, Roger Vanderwater wanted to speak with him in person about the berries.

The slave who could write tottered his dying body across the wonderful room and knelt by the couch of Vanderwater, holding out before him the tray. Large, green leaves covered the top of the tray, and these the body-servant alongside whisked away so that Vanderwater could see. And Roger Vanderwater, propped upon his elbow, saw. He saw the fresh, wonderful fruit lying there like precious jewels, and in the midst of it the arm of Tom Dixon as it had been torn from his body, well-washed, of course, my brothers, and very white against the blood-red fruit. And also he saw, clutched in the stiff, dead fingers, the petition of his slaves who toiled in Hell's Bottom.

"Take and read," said the slave who could write. And even as the master took the petition, the body-servant, who till then had been motionless with surprise, struck with his fist the kneeling slave upon the mouth. The slave was dying anyway, and was very weak, and did not mind. He made no sound, and, having fallen over on his side, he lay there quietly, bleeding from the blow on the mouth. The physician, who had run for the palace guards, came back with them, and the slave was dragged upright upon his feet. But as they dragged him up, his hand clutched Tom Dixon's arm from where it had fallen on the floor.

"He shall be flung alive to the hounds!" the body-servant was crying in great wrath. "He shall be flung alive to the hounds!"

But Roger Vanderwater, forgetting his headache, still leaning on his elbow, commanded silence, and went on reading the petition. And while he read, there was silence, all standing upright, the wrathful body-servant, the physician, the palace guards, and in their midst the slave, bleeding at the mouth and still holding Tom Dixon's arm. And when Roger Vanderwater had done, he turned upon the slave, saying:—

"If in this paper there be one lie, you shall be sorry that you were ever born."

And the slave said, "I have been sorry all my life that I was born."

Roger Vanderwater looked at him closely, and the slave said:—

"You have done your worst to me. I am dying now. In a week I shall be dead, so it does not matter if you kill me now."

"What do you with that?" the master asked, pointing to the arm; and the slave made answer:—

"I take it back to the pen to give it burial. Tom Dixon was my friend. We worked beside each other at our looms."

There is little more to my tale, brothers. The slave and the arm were sent back in a cart to the pen. Nor were any of the slaves punished for what they had done. Instead, Roger Vanderwater made investigation and punished the two overseers, Joseph Clancy and Adolph Munster. Their freeholds were taken from them. They were branded, each upon the forehead, their right hands were cut off, and they were turned loose upon the highway to wander and beg until they died. And the fund was managed rightfully thereafter for a time—for a time, only, my brothers; for after Roger Vanderwater came his son, Albert, who was a cruel master and half mad.

Brothers, that slave who carried the arm into the presence of the master was my father. He was a brave man. And even as his mother secretly taught him to read, so did he teach me. Because he died shortly after from the pick-handle beating, Roger Vanderwater took me out of the slave pen and tried to make various better things out of me. I might have become an overseer in Hell's Bottom, but I chose to become a story-teller, wandering over the land and getting close to my brothers, the slaves, everywhere. And I tell you stories like this, secretly, knowing that you will not betray me; for if you did, you know as well as I that my tongue will be torn out and that I shall tell stories no more. And my message is, brothers, that there is a good time coming, when all will be well in the world and there will be neither masters nor slaves. But first you must prepare for that good time by learning to read. There is power in the printed word. And here am I to teach you to read, and as well there are others to see that you get the books when I am gone along upon my way—the history books wherein you will learn about your masters, and learn to become strong even as they.

[EDITOR'S NOTE.—*From "Historical Fragments and Sketches" first published in fifty volumes in 4427, and now, after two hundred years, because of its accuracy and value, edited and republished by the National Committee on Historical Research.*]

A PIECE OF STEAK

With the last morsel of bread Tom King wiped his plate clean of the last particle of flour gravy and chewed the resulting mouthful in a slow and meditative way. When he arose from the table, he was oppressed by the feeling that he was distinctly hungry. Yet he alone had eaten. The two children in the other room had been sent early to bed in order that in sleep they might forget they had gone supperless. His wife had touched nothing, and had sat silently and watched him with solicitous eyes. She was a thin, worn woman of the working-class, though signs of an earlier prettiness were not wanting in her face. The flour for the gravy she had borrowed from the neighbor across the hall. The last two ha'pennies had gone to buy the bread.

He sat down by the window on a rickety chair that protested under his weight, and quite mechanically he put his pipe in his mouth and dipped into the side pocket of his coat. The absence of any tobacco made him aware of his action, and, with a scowl for his forgetfulness, he put the pipe away. His movements were slow, almost hulking, as though he were burdened by the heavy weight of his muscles. He was a solid-bodied, stolid-looking man, and his appearance did not suffer from being overprepossessing. His rough clothes were old and slouchy. The uppers of his shoes were too weak to carry the heavy resoling that was itself of no recent date. And his cotton shirt, a cheap, two-shilling affair, showed a frayed collar and ineradicable paint stains.

But it was Tom King's face that advertised him unmistakably for what he was. It was the face of a typical prize-fighter; of one who had put in long years of service in the squared ring and, by that means, developed and emphasized all the marks of the fighting beast. It was distinctly a lowering countenance, and, that no feature of it might escape notice, it was clean-shaven. The lips were shapeless, and constituted a mouth harsh to excess, that was like a gash in his face. The jaw was aggressive, brutal, heavy. The eyes, slow of movement and heavy-lidded, were almost expressionless under the shaggy, indrawn brows. Sheer animal that he was, the eyes were the most animal-like feature about him. They were sleepy, lion-like—the eyes of a fighting animal. The forehead slanted quickly back to the hair, which, clipped close, showed every bump of a villainous-looking head. A nose, twice broken and moulded variously by countless blows, and a cauliflower ear, permanently swollen and distorted to twice its size, completed his adornment, while the beard, fresh-shaven as it was, sprouted in the skin and gave the face a blue-black stain.

All together, it was the face of a man to be afraid of in a dark alley or lonely place. And yet Tom King was not a criminal, nor had he ever done anything criminal. Outside of brawls, common to his walk in life, he had harmed no one. Nor had he ever been known to pick a quarrel. He was a professional, and all the fighting brutishness of him was reserved for his professional appearances. Outside the ring he was slow-going, easy-natured, and, in his younger days, when money was flush, too open-handed for his own good. He bore no grudges and had few enemies. Fighting was a business with him. In the ring he struck to hurt, struck to maim, struck to destroy; but there was no animus in it. It was a plain business proposition. Audiences assembled and paid for the spectacle of men knocking each other out. The winner took the big end of the purse. When Tom King faced the Wool loomoolloo Gouger, twenty years before, he knew that the Gouger's jaw was only four months healed after having been broken in a Newcastle bout. And he had played for that jaw and broken it again in the ninth round, not because he bore the Gouger any ill-will, but because that was the surest way to put the Gouger out and win the big end of the purse. Nor had the Gouger borne him any ill-will for it. It was the game, and both knew the game and played it.

Tom King had never been a talker, and he sat by the window, morosely silent, staring at his hands. The veins stood out on the backs of the hands, large and swollen; and the knuckles, smashed and battered and malformed, testified to the use to which they had been put. He had never heard that a man's life was the life of his arteries, but well he knew the meaning of those big, upstanding veins. His heart had pumped too much blood through them at top pressure. They no longer did the work. He had stretched the elasticity out of them, and with their distention had passed his endurance. He tired easily now. No longer could he do a fast twenty rounds, hammer and tongs, fight, fight, fight, from gong to gong, with fierce rally on top of fierce rally, beaten to the ropes and in turn beating his opponent to the ropes, and rallying fiercest and fastest of all in that last, twentieth round, with the house on its feet and yelling, himself rushing, striking, ducking, raining showers of blows upon showers of blows and receiving showers of blows in return, and all the time the heart faithfully pumping the surging blood through the adequate veins. The veins, swollen at the time, had always shrunk down again, though not quite—each time, imperceptibly at first, remaining just a trifle larger than before. He stared at them and at his battered knuckles, and, for the moment, caught a vision of the youthful excellence of those hands before the first knuckle had been smashed on the head of Benny Jones, otherwise known as the Welsh Terror.

The impression of his hunger came back on him.

"Blimey, but couldn't I go a piece of steak!" he muttered aloud, clenching his huge fists and spitting out a smothered oath.

"I tried both Burke's an' Sawley's," his wife said half apologetically.

"An' they wouldn't?" he demanded.

"Not a ha'penny. Burke said—" She faltered.

"G'wan! Wot'd he say?"

"As how 'e was thinkin' Sandel ud do ye to-night, an' as how yer score was comfortable big as it was."

Tom King grunted, but did not reply. He was busy thinking of the bull terrier he had kept in his younger days to which he had fed steaks without end. Burke would have given him credit for a thousand steaks—then. But times had changed. Tom King was getting old; and old men, fighting before second-rate clubs, couldn't expect to run bills of any size with the tradesmen.

He had got up in the morning with a longing for a piece of steak, and the longing had not abated. He had not had a fair training for this fight. It was a drought year in Australia, times were hard, and even the most irregular work was difficult to find. He had had no sparring partner, and his food had not been of the best nor always sufficient. He had done a few days' navvy work when he could get it, and he had run around the Domain in the early mornings to get his legs in shape. But it was hard, training without a partner and with a wife and two kiddies that must be fed. Credit with the tradesmen had undergone very slight expansion when he was matched with Sandel. The secretary of the Gayety Club had advanced him three pounds—the loser's end of the purse—and beyond that had refused to go. Now and again he had managed to borrow a few shillings from old pals, who would have lent more only that it was a drought year and they were hard put themselves. No—and there was no use in disguising the fact—his training had not been satisfactory. He should have had better food and no worries. Besides, when a man is forty, it is harder to get into condition than when he is twenty.

"What time is it, Lizzie?" he asked.

His wife went across the hall to inquire, and came back.

"Quarter before eight."

"They'll be startin' the first bout in a few minutes," he said. "Only a try-out. Then there's a four-round spar 'tween Dealer Wells an' Gridley, an' a ten-round go 'tween Starlight an' some sailor bloke. I don't come on for over an hour."

At the end of another silent ten minutes, he rose to his feet.

"Truth is, Lizzie, I ain't had proper trainin'."

He reached for his hat and started for the door. He did not offer to kiss her—he never did on going out—but on this night she dared to kiss him, throwing her arms around him and compelling him to bend down to her face. She looked quite small against the massive bulk of the man.

"Good luck, Tom," she said. "You gotter do 'im."

"Ay, I gotter do 'im," he repeated. "That's all there is to it. I jus' gotter do 'im."

He laughed with an attempt at heartiness, while she pressed more closely against him. Across her shoulders he looked around the bare room. It was all he had in the world, with the rent overdue, and her and the kiddies. And he was leaving it to go out into the night to get meat for his mate and cubs—not like a modern working-man going to his machine grind, but in the old, primitive, royal, animal way, by fighting for it.

"I gotter do 'im," he repeated, this time a hint of desperation in his voice. "If it's a win, it's thirty quid—an' I can pay all that's owin', with a lump o' money left over. If it's a lose, I get naught—not even a penny for me to ride home on the tram. The secretary's give all that's comin' from a loser's end. Good-by, old woman. I'll come straight home if it's a win."

"An' I'll be waitin' up," she called to him along the hall.

It was full two miles to the Gayety, and as he walked along he remembered how in his palmy days—he had once been the heavy-weight champion of New South Wales—he would have ridden in a cab to the fight, and how, most likely, some heavy backer would have paid for the cab and ridden with him. There were Tommy Burns and that Yankee nigger, Jack Johnson—they rode about in motor-cars. And he walked! And, as any man knew, a hard two miles was not the best preliminary to a fight. He was an old un, and the world did not wag well with old uns. He was good for nothing now except navvy work, and his broken nose and swollen ear were against him even in that. He found himself wishing that he had learned a trade. It would have been better in the long run. But no one had told him, and he knew, deep down in his heart, that he would not have listened if they had. It had been so easy. Big money—sharp, glorious fights—periods of rest and loafing in between—a following of eager flatterers, the slaps on the back, the shakes of the hand, the toffs glad to buy him a drink for the privilege of five minutes' talk—and the glory of it, the yelling houses, the whirlwind finish, the referee's "King wins!" and his name in the sporting columns next day.

Those had been times! But he realized now, in his slow, ruminating way, that it was the old uns he had been putting away. He was Youth, rising; and they were Age, sinking. No wonder it had been easy—they with their swollen veins and battered knuckles and weary in the bones of them from the long battles they had already fought. He remembered the time he put out old Stowsher Bill, at Rush-Cutters Bay, in the eighteenth round, and how old Bill had cried afterward in the dressing-room like a baby. Perhaps old Bill's rent had been overdue. Perhaps he'd had at home a missus an' a couple of kiddies. And perhaps Bill, that very day of the fight, had had a hungering for a piece of steak. Bill had fought game and taken incredible punishment. He could see now, after he had gone through the mill himself, that Stowsher Bill had fought for a bigger stake, that night twenty years ago, than had young Tom King, who had fought for glory and easy money. No wonder Stowsher Bill had cried afterward in the dressing-room.

Well, a man had only so many fights in him, to begin with. It was the iron law of the game. One man might have a hundred hard fights in him, another man only twenty; each, according to the make of him and the quality of his fibre, had a definite number, and, when he had fought them, he was done. Yes, he had had more fights in him than most of them, and he had had far more than his share of the hard, gruelling fights—the kind that worked the heart and lungs to bursting, that took the elastic out of the arteries and made hard knots of muscle out of Youth's sleek suppleness, that wore out nerve and stamina and made brain and bones weary from excess of effort and endurance overwrought. Yes, he had done better than all of them. There was none of his old fighting partners left. He was the last of the old guard. He had seen them all finished, and he had had a hand in finishing some of them.

They had tried him out against the old uns, and

one after another he had put them away—laughing when, like old Stowsher Bill, they cried in the dressing-room. And now he was an old un, and they tried out the youngsters on him. There was that bloke, Sandel. He had come over from New Zealand with a record behind him. But nobody in Australia knew anything about him, so they put him up against old Tom King. If Sandel made a showing, he would be given better men to fight, with bigger purses to win; so it was to be depended upon that he would put up a fierce battle. He had everything to win by it—money and glory and career; and Tom King was the grizzled old chopping-block that guarded the highway to fame and fortune. And he had nothing to win except thirty quid, to pay to the landlord and the tradesmen. And, as Tom King thus ruminated, there came to his stolid vision the form of Youth, glorious Youth, rising exultant and invincible, supple of muscle and silken of skin, with heart and lungs that had never been tired and torn and that laughed at limitation of effort. Yes, Youth was the Nemesis. It destroyed the old uns and recked not that, in so doing, it destroyed itself. It enlarged its arteries and smashed its knuckles, and was in turn destroyed by Youth. For Youth was ever youthful. It was only Age that grew old.

At Castlereagh Street he turned to the left, and three blocks along came to the Gayety. A crowd of young larrikins hanging outside the door made respectful way for him, and he heard one say to another: "That's 'im! That's Tom King!"

Inside, on the way to his dressing-room, he encountered the secretary, a keen-eyed, shrewd-faced young man, who shook his hand.

"How are you feelin', Tom?" he asked.

"Fit as a fiddle," King answered, though he knew that he lied, and that if he had a quid, he would give it right there for a good piece of steak.

When he emerged from the dressing-room, his seconds behind him, and came down the aisle to the squared ring in the centre of the hall, a burst of greeting and applause went up from the waiting crowd. He acknowledged salutations right and left, though few of the faces did he know. Most of them were the faces of kiddies unborn when he was winning his first laurels in the squared ring. He leaped lightly to the raised platform and ducked through the ropes to his corner, where he sat down on a folding stool. Jack Ball, the referee, came over and shook his hand. Ball was a broken-down pugilist who for over ten years had not entered the ring as a principal. King was glad that he had him for referee. They were both old uns. If he should rough it with Sandel a bit beyond the rules, he knew Ball could be depended upon to pass it by.

Aspiring young heavyweights, one after another, were climbing into the ring and being presented to the audience by the referee. Also, he issued their challenges for them.

"Young Pronto," Bill announced, "from North Sydney, challenges the winner for fifty pounds side bet."

The audience applauded, and applauded again as Sandel himself sprang through the ropes and sat down in his corner. Tom King looked across the ring at him curiously, for in a few minutes they would be locked together in merciless combat, each trying with all the force of him to knock the other into unconsciousness. But little could he see, for Sandel, like himself, had trousers and sweater on over his ring costume. His face was strongly handsome, crowned with a curly mop of yellow hair, while his thick, muscular neck hinted at bodily magnificence.

Young Pronto went to one corner and then the other, shaking hands with the principals and dropping down out of the ring. The challenges went on. Ever Youth climbed through the ropes—Youth unknown, but insatiable—crying out to mankind that with strength and skill it would match issues with the winner. A few years before, in his own heyday of invincibleness, Tom King would have been amused and bored by these preliminaries. But now he sat fascinated, unable to shake the vision of Youth from his eyes. Always were these youngsters rising up in the boxing game, springing through the ropes and shouting their defiance; and always were the old uns going down before them. They climbed to success over the bodies of the old uns. And ever they came, more and more youngsters—Youth unquenchable and irresistible—and ever they put the old uns away, themselves becoming old uns and travelling the same downward path, while behind them, ever pressing on them, was Youth eternal— the new babies, grown lusty and dragging their elders down, with behind them more babies to the end of time—Youth that must have its will and that will never die.

King glanced over to the press box and nodded to Morgan, of the *Sportsman,* and Corbett, of the *Referee.* Then he held out his hands, while Sid Sullivan and Charley Bates, his seconds, slipped on his gloves and laced them tight, closely watched by one of Sandel's seconds, who first examined critically the tapes on King's knuckles. A second of his own was in Sandel's corner, performing a like office. Sandel's trousers were pulled off, and, as he stood up, his sweater was skinned off over his head. And Tom King, looking, saw Youth incarnate, deep-chested, heavy-thewed, with muscles that slipped and slid like live things under the white satin skin. The whole body was acrawl with life, and Tom King knew that it was a life that had never oozed its freshness out through the aching pores during the long fights wherein Youth paid its toll and departed not quite so young as when it entered.

The two men advanced to meet each other, and, as the gong sounded and the seconds clattered out of the ring with the folding stools, they shook hands and instantly took their fighting attitudes. And instantly, like a mechanism of steel and springs balanced on a hair trigger, Sandel was in and out and in again, landing a left to the eyes, a right to the ribs, ducking a counter, dancing lightly away and dancing menacingly back again. He was swift and clever. It was a dazzling exhibition. The house yelled its approbation. But King was not dazzled. He had fought too many fights and too many youngsters. He knew the blows for what they were—too quick and too deft to be dangerous. Evidently Sandel was going to rush things from the start. It was to be expected. It was the way of Youth, expending its splendor and excellence in wild insurgence and furious onslaught, overwhelming opposition with its own unlimited glory of strength and desire.

Sandel was in and out, here, there, and everywhere, light-footed and eager-hearted, a living wonder of white flesh and stinging muscle that wove itself into a dazzling fabric of attack, slipping and leaping like a flying shuttle from action to action through a thousand actions, all of them centred upon the destruction of Tom King, who stood between him and fortune. And Tom King patiently endured. He knew his business, and he knew Youth now that Youth was no longer his. There was nothing to do till the other lost some of his steam, was his thought, and he grinned to himself as he deliberately ducked so as to receive a heavy blow on the top of his head. It was a wicked thing to do, yet eminently fair according to the rules of the boxing game. A man was supposed to take care of his own knuckles, and, if he insisted on hitting an opponent on the top of the head, he did so at his own peril. King could have ducked lower and let the blow whiz harmlessly past, but he remembered his own early fights and how he smashed his first knuckle on the head of the Welsh Terror. He was but playing the game. That duck had accounted for one of Sandel's knuckles. Not that Sandel would mind it now. He would go on, superbly regardless, hitting as hard as ever throughout the fight. But later on, when the long ring battles had begun to tell, he would regret that knuckle and look back and remember how he smashed it on Tom King's head.

The first round was all Sandel's, and he had the house yelling with the rapidity of his whirlwind rushes. He overwhelmed King with avalanches of punches, and King did nothing. He never struck once, contenting himself with covering up, blocking and ducking and clinching to avoid punishment. He occasionally feinted, shook his head when the weight of a punch landed, and moved stolidly about, never leaping or springing or wasting an ounce of strength. Sandel must foam the froth of Youth away before discreet Age could dare to retaliate. All King's movements were slow and methodical, and his heavy-lidded, slow-moving eyes gave him the appearance of being half asleep or dazed. Yet they were eyes that saw everything, that had been trained to see everything through all his twenty years and odd in the ring. They were eyes that did not blink or waver before an impending blow, but that coolly saw and measured distance.

Seated in his corner for the minute's rest at the end of the round, he lay back with outstretched legs, his arms resting on the right angle of the ropes, his chest and abdomen heaving frankly and deeply as he gulped down the air driven by the towels of his seconds. He listened with closed eyes to the voices of the house, "Why don't yeh fight, Tom?" many were crying. "Yeh ain't afraid of 'im, are yeh?"

"Muscle-bound," he heard a man on a front seat comment. "He can't move quicker. Two to one on Sandel, in quids."

The gong struck and the two men advanced from their corners. Sandel came forward fully three-quarters of the distance, eager to begin again; but King was content to advance the shorter distance. It was in line with his policy of economy. He had not been well trained, and he had not had enough to eat, and every step counted. Besides, he had already walked two miles to the ringside. It was a repetition of the first round, with Sandel attacking like a whirlwind and with the audience indignantly demanding why King did not fight. Beyond feinting and several slowly delivered and ineffectual blows he did nothing save block and stall and clinch. Sandel wanted to make the pace fast, while King, out of his wisdom, refused to accommodate him. He grinned with a certain wistful pathos in his ring-battered countenance, and went on cherishing his strength with the jealousy of which only Age is capable. Sandel was Youth, and he threw his strength away with the munificent abandon of Youth. To King belonged the ring generalship, the wisdom bred of long, aching fights. He watched with cool eyes and head, moving slowly and waiting for Sandel's froth to foam away. To the majority of the onlookers it seemed as though King was hopelessly outclassed, and they voiced their opinion in offers of three to one on Sandel. But there were wise ones, a few, who knew King of old time, and who covered what they considered easy money.

The third round began as usual, one-sided, with Sandel doing all the leading and delivering all the punishment. A half-minute had passed when Sandel, overconfident, left an opening. King's eyes and right arm flashed in the same instant. It was his first real blow—a hook, with the twisted arch of the arm to make it rigid, and with all the weight of the half-pivoted body behind it. It was like a sleepy-seeming lion suddenly thrusting out a lightning paw. Sandel, caught on the side of the jaw, was felled like a bullock. The audience gasped and murmured awe-stricken applause. The man was not muscle-bound, after all, and he could drive a blow like a trip-hammer.

Sandel was shaken. He rolled over and attempted to rise, but the sharp yells from his seconds to take the count restrained him. He knelt on one knee, ready to rise, and waited, while the referee stood over him, counting the seconds loudly in his ear. At the ninth he rose in fighting attitude, and Tom King, facing him, knew regret that the blow had not been an inch nearer the point of the jaw. That would have been a knockout, and he could have carried the thirty quid home to the missus and the kiddies.

The round continued to the end of its three minutes, Sandel for the first time respectful of his opponent and King slow of movement and sleepy-eyed as ever. As the round neared its close, King, warned of the fact by sight of the seconds crouching outside ready for the spring in through the ropes, worked the fight around to his own corner. And when the gong struck, he sat down immediately on the waiting stool, while Sandel had to walk all the way across the diagonal of the square to his own corner. It was a little thing, but it was the sum of little things that counted. Sandel was compelled to walk that many more steps, to give up that much energy, and to lose a part of the precious minute of rest. At the beginning of every round King loafed slowly out from his corner, forcing his opponent to advance the greater distance. The end of every round found the fight manœuvred by King into his own corner so that he could immediately sit down.

Two more rounds went by, in which King was parsimonious of effort and Sandel prodigal. The latter's attempt to force a fast pace made King un-comfortable, for a fair percentage of the multitudi-nous blows showered upon him went home. Yet King persisted in his dogged slowness, despite the crying of the young hotheads for him to go in and fight. Again, in the sixth round, Sandel was careless, again Tom King's fearful right flashed out to the jaw, and again Sandel took the nine seconds count.

By the seventh round Sandel's pink of condition was gone, and he settled down to what he knew was to be the hardest fight in his experience. Tom King was an old un, but a better old un than he had ever encountered—an old un who never lost his head, who was remarkably able at defence, whose blows had the impact of a knotted club, and who had a knockout in either hand. Nevertheless, Tom King dared not hit often. He never forgot his battered knuckles, and knew that every hit must count if the knuckles were to last out the fight. As he sat in his corner, glancing across at his opponent, the thought came to him that the sum of his wisdom and Sandel's youth would constitute a world's champion heavyweight. But that was the trouble. Sandel would never become a world champion. He lacked the wisdom, and the only way for him to get it was to buy it with Youth; and when wisdom was his, Youth would have been spent in buying it.

King took every advantage he knew. He never missed an opportunity to clinch, and in effecting most of the clinches his shoulder drove stiffly into the other's ribs. In the philosophy of the ring a shoulder was as good as a punch so far as damage was concerned, and a great deal better so far as concerned expenditure of effort. Also, in the clinches King rested his weight on his opponent, and was loath to let go. This compelled the interference of the referee, who tore them apart, always assisted by Sandel, who had not yet learned to rest. He could not refrain from using those glorious flying arms and writhing muscles of his, and when the other rushed into a clinch, striking shoulder against ribs, and with head resting under Sandel's left arm, Sandel almost invariably swung his right behind his own back and into the projecting face. It was a clever stroke, much admired by the audience, but it was not dangerous, and was, therefore, just that much wasted strength. But Sandel was tireless and unaware of limitations, and King grinned and doggedly endured.

A Piece of Steak

Sandel developed a fierce right to the body, which made it appear that King was taking an enormous amount of punishment, and it was only the old ringsters who appreciated the deft touch of King's left glove to the other's biceps just before the impact of the blow. It was true, the blow landed each time; but each time it was robbed of its power by that touch on the biceps. In the ninth round, three times inside a minute, King's right hooked its twisted arch to the jaw; and three times Sandel's body, heavy as it was, was levelled to the mat. Each time he took the nine seconds allowed him and rose to his feet, shaken and jarred, but still strong. He had lost much of his speed, and he wasted less effort. He was fighting grimly; but he continued to draw upon his chief asset, which was Youth. King's chief asset was experience. As his vitality had dimmed and his vigor abated, he had replaced them with cunning, with wisdom born of the long fights and with a careful shepherding of strength. Not alone had he learned never to make a superfluous movement, but he had learned how to seduce an opponent into throwing his strength away. Again and again, by feint of foot and hand and body he continued to inveigle Sandel into leaping back, ducking, or countering. King rested, but he never permitted Sandel to rest. It was the strategy of Age.

Early in the tenth round King began stopping the other's rushes with straight lefts to the face, and Sandel, grown wary, responded by drawing the left, then by ducking it and delivering his right in a swinging hook to the side of the head. It was too high up to be vitally effective; but when first it landed, King knew the old, familiar descent of the black veil of unconsciousness across his mind. For the instant, or for the slightest fraction of an instant, rather, he ceased. In the one moment he saw his opponent ducking out of his field of vision and the background of white, watching faces; in the next moment he again saw his opponent and the background of faces. It was as if he had slept for a time and just opened his eyes again, and yet the interval of unconsciousness was so microscopically short that there had been no time for him to fall. The audience saw him totter and his knees give, and then saw him recover and tuck his chin deeper into the shelter of his left shoulder.

Several times Sandel repeated the blow, keeping

King partially dazed, and then the latter worked out his defence, which was also a counter. Feinting with his left he took a half-step backward, at the same time upper cutting with the whole strength of his right. So accurately was it timed that it landed squarely on Sandel's face in the full, downward sweep of the duck, and Sandel lifted in the air and curled backward, striking the mat on his head and shoulders. Twice King achieved this, then turned loose and hammered his opponent to the ropes. He gave Sandel no chance to rest or to set himself, but smashed blow in upon blow till the house rose to its feet and the air was filled with an unbroken roar of applause. But Sandel's strength and endurance were superb, and he continued to stay on his feet. A knockout seemed certain, and a captain of police, appalled at the dreadful punishment, arose by the ringside to stop the fight. The gong struck for the end of the round and Sandel staggered to his corner, protesting to the captain that he was sound and strong. To prove it, he threw two back air-springs, and the police captain gave in.

Tom King, leaning back in his corner and breathing hard, was disappointed. If the fight had been stopped, the referee, perforce, would have rendered him the decision and the purse would have been his. Unlike Sandel, he was not fighting for glory or career, but for thirty quid. And now Sandel would recuperate in the minute of rest.

Youth will be served—this saying flashed into King's mind, and he remembered the first time he had heard it, the night when he had put away Stowsher Bill. The toff who had bought him a drink after the fight and patted him on the shoulder had used those words. Youth will be served! The toff was right. And on that night in the long ago he had been Youth. To-night Youth sat in the opposite corner. As for himself, he had been fighting for half an hour now, and he was an old man. Had he fought like Sandel, he would not have lasted fifteen minutes. But the point was that he did not recuperate. Those upstanding arteries and that sorely tried heart would not enable him to gather strength in the intervals between the rounds. And he had not had sufficient strength in him to begin with. His legs were heavy under him and beginning to cramp. He should not have walked those two miles to the fight. And there was the steak which he had got up longing for that morning. A great and terrible hatred rose up in him for the butchers who had refused him credit. It was hard for an old man to go into a fight without enough to eat. And a piece of steak was such a little thing, a few pennies at best; yet it meant thirty quid to him.

With the gong that opened the eleventh round, Sandel rushed, making a show of freshness which he did not really possess. King knew it for what it was— a bluff as old as the game itself. He clinched to save himself, then, going free, allowed Sandel to get set. This was what King desired. He feinted with his left, drew the answering duck and swinging upward hook, then made the half-step backward, delivered the upper cut full to the face and crumpled Sandel over to the mat. After that he never let him rest, receiving punishment himself, but inflicting far more, smashing Sandel to the ropes, hooking and driving all manner of blows into him, tearing away from his clinches or punching him out of attempted clinches, and ever when Sandel would have fallen, catching him with one uplifting hand and with the other immediately smashing him into the ropes where he could not fall.

The house by this time had gone mad, and it was his house, nearly every voice yelling: "Go it, Tom!" "Get 'im! Get 'im!" "You've got 'im, Tom! You've got 'im!" It was to be a whirlwind finish, and that was what a ringside audience paid to see.

And Tom King, who for half an hour had conserved his strength, now expended it prodigally in the one great effort he knew he had in him. It was his one chance—now or not at all. His strength was waning fast, and his hope was that before the last of it ebbed out of him he would have beaten his opponent down for the count. And as he continued to strike and force, coolly estimating the weight of his blows and the quality of the damage wrought, he realized how hard a man Sandel was to knock out. Stamina and endurance were his to an extreme degree, and they were the virgin stamina and endurance of Youth. Sandel was certainly a coming man. He had it in him. Only out of such rugged fibre were successful fighters fashioned.

Sandel was reeling and staggering, but Tom King's legs were cramping and his knuckles going back on him. Yet he steeled himself to strike the fierce blows, every one of which brought anguish to his tortured hands. Though now he was receiving practically no punishment, he was weakening as rapidly as the other. His blows went home, but there was no longer the weight behind them, and each blow was the result of a severe effort of will. His legs were like lead, and they dragged visibly under him; while Sandel's backers, cheered by this symptom, began calling encouragement to their man.

King was spurred to a burst of effort. He delivered two blows in succession—a left, a trifle too high, to the solar plexus, and a right cross to the jaw. They were not heavy blows, yet so weak and dazed was Sandel that he went down and lay quivering. The referee stood over him, shouting the count of the fatal seconds in his ear. If before the tenth second was called, he did not rise, the fight was lost. The house stood in hushed silence. King rested on trembling legs. A mortal dizziness was upon him, and before his eyes the sea of faces sagged and swayed, while to his ears, as from a remote distance, came the count of the referee. Yet he looked upon the fight as his. It was impossible that a man so punished could rise.

Only Youth could rise, and Sandel rose. At the

fourth second he rolled over on his face and groped blindly for the ropes. By the seventh second he had dragged himself to his knee, where he rested, his head rolling groggily on his shoulders. As the referee cried "Nine!" Sandel stood upright, in proper stalling position, his left arm wrapped about his face, his right wrapped about his stomach. Thus were his vital points guarded, while he lurched forward toward King in the hope of effecting a clinch and gaining more time.

At the instant Sandel arose, King was at him, but the two blows he delivered were muffled on the stalled arms. The next moment Sandel was in the clinch and holding on desperately while the referee strove to drag the two men apart. King helped to force himself free. He knew the rapidity with which Youth recovered, and he knew that Sandel was his if he could prevent that recovery. One stiff punch would do it. Sandel was his, indubitably his. He had outgeneralled him, outfought him, outpointed him. Sandel reeled out of the clinch, balanced on the hair line between defeat or survival. One good blow would topple him over and down and out. And Tom King, in a flash of bitterness, remembered the piece of steak and wished that he had it then behind that necessary punch he must deliver. He nerved himself for the blow, but it was not heavy enough nor swift enough. Sandel swayed, but did not fall, staggering back to the ropes and holding on. King staggered after him, and, with a pang like that of dissolution, delivered another blow. But his body had deserted him. All that was left of him was a fighting intelligence that was dimmed and clouded from exhaustion. The blow that was aimed for the jaw struck no higher than the shoulder. He had willed the blow higher, but the tired muscles had not been able to obey. And, from the impact of the blow, Tom King himself reeled back and nearly fell. Once again he strove. This time his punch missed altogether, and, from absolute weakness, he fell against Sandel and clinched, holding on to him to save himself from sinking to the floor.

King did not attempt to free himself. He had shot his bolt. He was gone. And Youth had been served. Even in the clinch he could feel Sandel growing stronger against him. When the referee thrust them apart, there, before his eyes, he saw Youth recuperate. From instant to instant Sandel grew stronger.

His punches, weak and futile at first, became stiff and accurate. Tom King's bleared eyes saw the gloved fist driving at his jaw, and he willed to guard it by interposing his arm. He saw the danger, willed the act; but the arm was too heavy. It seemed burdened with a hundredweight of lead. It would not lift itself, and he strove to lift it with his soul. Then the gloved fist landed home. He experienced a sharp snap that was like an electric spark, and, simultaneously, the veil of blackness enveloped him.

When he opened his eyes again he was in his corner, and he heard the yelling of the audience like the roar of the surf at Bondi Beach. A wet sponge was being pressed against the base of his brain, and Sid Sullivan was blowing cold water in a refreshing spray over his face and chest. His gloves had already been removed, and Sandel, bending over him, was shaking his hand. He bore no ill-will toward the man who had put him out, and he returned the grip with a heartiness that made his battered knuckles protest. Then Sandel stepped to the centre of the ring and the audience hushed its pandemonium to hear him accept young Pronto's challenge and offer to increase the side bet to one hundred pounds. King looked on apathetically while his seconds mopped the streaming water from him, dried his face, and prepared him to leave the ring. He felt hungry. It was not the ordinary, gnawing kind, but a great faintness, a palpitation at the pit of the stomach that communicated itself to all his body. He remembered back into the fight to the moment when he had Sandel swaying and tottering on the hair-line balance of defeat. Ah, that piece of steak would have done it! He had lacked just that for the decisive blow, and he had lost. It was all because of the piece of steak.

His seconds were half-supporting him as they helped him through the ropes. He tore free from them, ducked through the ropes unaided, and leaped heavily to the floor, following on their heels as they forced a passage for him down the crowded centre aisle. Leaving the dressing-room for the street, in the entrance to the hall, some young fellow spoke to him.

"W'y didn't yuh go in an' get 'im when yuh 'ad 'im?" the young fellow asked.

"Aw, go to hell!" said Tom King, and passed down the steps to the sidewalk.

The doors of the public house at the corner were

swinging wide, and he saw the lights and the smiling barmaids, heard the many voices discussing the fight and the prosperous chink of money on the bar. Somebody called to him to have a drink. He hesitated perceptibly, then refused and went on his way.

He had not a copper in his pocket, and the two-mile walk home seemed very long. He was certainly getting old. Crossing the Domain, he sat down suddenly on a bench, unnerved by the thought of the missus sitting up for him, waiting to learn the outcome of the fight. That was harder than any knockout, and it seemed almost impossible to face.

He felt weak and sore, and the pain of his smashed knuckles warned him that, even if he could find a job at navvy work, it would be a week before he could grip a pick handle or a shovel. The hunger palpitation at the pit of the stomach was sickening. His wretchedness overwhelmed him, and into his eyes came an unwonted moisture. He covered his face with his hands, and, as he cried, he remembered Stowsher Bill and how he had served him that night in the long ago. Poor old Stowsher Bill! He could understand now why Bill had cried in the dressing-room.